I0445767

VICE RIDE

A FLAWED ATTRACTIONS ROMANCE

MJ MOORES

Love Nest Books

VICE RIDE
MJ MOORES

Love Knot Books

https://loveknotbooks.ca

Love Knot Books is an imprint of DAOwen Publications
Copyright © MJ Moores
All rights reserved

DAOwen Publications supports copyright. Copyright fuels creativity, encourages diverse voices, promotes free speech, and creates a vibrant culture. Thank you for buying an authorized edition of this book and for complying with copyright laws by not reproducing, scanning, or distributing any part of it in any form without permission. You are supporting writers and allowing DAOwen Publications to continue to publish books for every reader.

Vice Ride / MJ Moores

Edited by Douglas Owen and Miles Cruise

This is a work of fiction. Names, characters, places, and incidents either are the product of the author's imagination or are used fictitiously, and any resemblance to actual persons, living or dead, businesses, companies, events, or locales is entirely coincidental.

Cover art by MMT Productions and Infinite Pathways

ISBN 978-1-928094-60-9
EISBN 978-1-928094-61-6

10 9 8 7 6 5 4 3 2 1

ACKNOWLEDGEMENTS

When you're building a world and a story, in general, there are always key people who help bolster and refine and advise along the way. These people are my early readers/beta readers, my writing buddy, my critique groups (yes, I have multiple), support groups (anti-procrastination peeps) and my editor.

With Vice Ride, though, I needed a little extra help. The police get involved in the storyline in a very specific way, and I required insight from multiple sources to help with the realism and believability of these scenes. I would like to thank Police Constable David Hopkins with the Toronto Police Services Media Relations, my dear cousin Chantelle (a Dispatcher) and her formidable husband Matt (a Police Constable) for providing me with the information I needed and didn't look at me like I was crazy for asking - lol!

I would also like to thank my colleague and research assistant Jan Richardson. Her "take no prisoners" and "dive right in" approach helped tremendously when my introverted and shy nature got the better of me.

I hope you enjoy Vice Ride, it was certainly a wild ride writing it.

MJ

1

VENUS FLY TRAP

Amber pulled her old three-door Mini into the driveway, shut off the engine, and dropped her forehead onto the steering wheel between pale hands. She couldn't make herself open the door – then it would be true. She'd be back for good.

Eyes shut tight, she held back a sigh. Her body shuddered. Swallowing her frustrations, Amber clenched the steering wheel before convincing herself to leave the vehicle. Her back and legs complained after two hours of driving. She stretched tall. The brisk January air hit her stomach under the waistband of her jacket and she shivered.

Amber yanked the bottom of her coat down and popped open the trunk. The porch light flickered on as a gust of wind brought a smattering of fat snowflakes. *Dad's home. I'm surprised. At least I can get this over with sooner.* Amber grabbed her oversized backpack, stuffed duffel bag, three large totes, and shuffled up the driveway to the house.

But the door didn't open.

"Oh, come on." She shifted to look through the tall pane of decorative-cut glass, trying to see through to the other side.

No one.

"I should've known." It wasn't like she'd told anyone she

was coming. The bags dropped from her shoulders to her elbows and then down onto the worn welcome mat that had sat on the porch, rain or shine, as far back as she could remember.

For laughs, she twisted the knob to see if he'd unlocked the door but hadn't waited. Nope. Locked. She glanced up at the light. *Must be on a timer. That's new.* Amber pushed a stray strand of hair behind her ear and jogged back to the trunk for the rest of her stuff.

She pried up the closest edge of the large bag, struggling to free the handle. Cold, stiff fingers gripped what little surface area she'd managed. Amber heaved and yanked and pulled. With each renewed effort, she claimed a little more real estate.

"Huh," the grunt snuck out with a final twist up. She staggered back, heaving the overstuffed suitcase as a counterbalance, tripped over her own feet, and stumbled to the bottom of the driveway. Somehow, Amber managed not to land on her ass with fifty pounds of clothes pinning her to the asphalt. A flicker of light caught her eye. She looked across the street, and her pride at catching herself plummeted below her knees.

A tall, narrow silhouette with broad shoulders watched her from the bay window. The person turned as if someone called. The light illuminated a familiar profile.

"Great." *Just freakin' great. So much for a quiet homecoming. So much for avoiding the biggest mistake of my life.* Amber's heart cinched. *No. He's not worth it.* She inhaled a deep breath and erased the ghost-ache...or tried to.

Josh turned back to the window. Amber couldn't say for sure he watched her, but she shivered under the weight of a stare she'd managed to avoid for the last eighteen months. And yet, it only felt like yesterday.

Shoving down the urge to give him the finger, she slammed the trunk, nabbed her keys, and hauled her luggage over to the porch. Even with Josh spying on her, Amber hesitated after shoving the house key into the lock.

I don't have to be here. No one asked me to come home. But then, no one would. Not outright. She'd fought so hard to get away. Going to school in London, Ontario, could have been London, England, without the accents and tiny roads, for all the communication she'd had with anyone back home. Etobicoke had dropped off the map for her. It was perfect. But nothing ever stayed that way.

Amber gave in to the sigh, resigned, and shouldered the door open, past the spot that rubbed. *Better to be out of the sight of prying eyes anyway.* She dragged her bags and totes into the lit foyer and shoved the door closed with her foot. Even having the solid barrier between her and the outside, a part of her knew *he* still watched the house. Tomorrow, everyone in town would know she was back – and that wasn't necessarily a good thing.

She shrugged her coat off and hung it from the knob on one of the bi-folding closet doors before heel-toeing her boots off and stepping into the dark house. Stomach grumbling, Amber switched on the kitchen light and stopped short. Her gaze swept over the dirty dishes piled in and beside the sink; pots and empty cans of soup and chilli lay on the stove and a single, used bowl and cup sat at her father's place at the table – his chair askew, not neatly pushed in like the other three. A dense bubble rose in her throat. She struggled to swallow.

Amber pushed herself to walk across a sticky floor and open the fridge: jar of pickles, carton of milk, half a loaf of bread, margarine, mayo, and an open stack of bologna. She yanked on the crisper and a bunch of apples rolled around.

"Oh, Dad. How can you take care of her if you can't even take care of yourself?"

Amber grabbed the pickle jar, nabbed one of the last two offerings, and held the end in her mouth as she screwed the lid back on. She slid the container back onto the shelf and shut the door before wiping her fingers on her jeans. Munching on the pathetic excuse for a dinner, Amber took the dish soap out of the cupboard and set it on the counter before emptying the sink of week-old dishes. It gave her something to think about besides being home. Or ass-hat Josh.

2
———

CLASH OF THE TITANS

The haze of sleep shifted. Amber stirred, wishing Nanci would quit making so much noise. They'd agreed to the dorm rules on day one and she had a bad habit of ignoring them. Amber rubbed her face, ready to complain, but a cramp in her foot and an all-too-familiar door scrape demanded she open her eyes. Her laptop, also asleep, sat open on her partially crossed legs. Light from the streetlamp outside cast a yellowish-orange hue across the back of the couch. *Not my dorm. Not my roommate.* She sat up and stretched a crick from her neck turning toward the sound. The small sofa pillow wasn't meant for napping.

"Amber," a deep, tired voice resonated.

A jolt of joy clashed with something much darker in her chest.

"Dad." She swung her legs over the edge of the couch, scattering segments of folded Penny Saver job ads. Neon pink highlighter circles popped like a disease over the tiny print.

"What are you doing here? Doesn't school start up again on Monday?" He set his briefcase down, took off his shoes, and slid off his jacket painfully slowly.

She snapped her laptop shut and set it on the coffee table.

"Yeah. I wanted to job hunt this weekend before the assignments roll in."

He rubbed his face with a hand and leaned his shoulder against the part-wall of the small foyer. "I don't understand. Why are you job hunting here? Isn't the scholarship enough? That and your summer earnings?"

Amber stood up. "No, it's not. I've transferred to Humber. I'm home." That one word hung in the soft glow of the night lights and red and green power lights for the TV and PVR. A hazy resonance from the new outside light filtered through the window of the front door washing out her father's features – or maybe he was just that pale.

"You've what?" His voice came sharp.

Amber stiffened, throwing up every mental barrier possible. Her father pushed off the wall and stood at his full height, imposing his presence and his unspoken opinions into the space.

"I've come home."

"No. You can't give up the scholarship just because I called you."

"You bloody bet I can. It's my choice. Just like it was my choice to leave in the first place."

"After everything we went through after high school, you're just giving up?" His voice rose, incredulous.

"I'm not giving up. I'm going to school at Humber now. For God's sake, Dad, you kept me in the dark for two weeks?"

"I didn't want it to interfere with your exams."

"To hell with my exams. Something like this they would have rescheduled them for me."

"It wasn't necessary. She's fine."

"She's not fine! She's in the goddamn hospital. When did me moving out equate to you not telling me what's going on?"

"I told you, it's not that bad. She has time."

"Clearly, it's bad enough that you're leaving open cans of food on the counter, stacks of dishes, and–"

"That's not important. Your education is. What is this move going to do to your studies?"

"Nothing. The Dean cleared all my courses. Everything's been transferred. I just don't have–"

"The scholarship. Are you really going to compromise your learning by working at the same time? Why didn't you discuss this with us? With me?"

"It's my life, my choice. What? Am I not welcome back home? Have you changed my room into a den without telling me? If you're out half the night, every night, at the hospital, then who's taking care of the house? You're not eating right. Look at you. You're exhausted. Are you working Saturdays again to pay for her meds? How do you plan on getting up in the morning when–"

"Enough! I'm making it work."

"And so am I!" She snatched up various papers, grabbed her laptop, and hugged the lot to her chest. "Stop keeping me in the dark," she said, and stormed down the hall to her room. Amber pushed her door open and kicked her bags inside before shutting the door with her foot. When she looked up, breathing hard, she froze. Her insides clenched tighter than before, stomach roiling. Amber hadn't slept at home for a year and a half. Not since she'd started at Fanshawe.

Her multi-hued pink duvet held her favourite stuffed animals where the bed met the wall; framed photos of her shaking the principal's hand littered the back of her desk; and a pile of folded clothes that never made it into her suitcase sat on the chair.

Nothing had changed.

Her room looked exactly as it had all those months ago; exactly as it had all through high school. *High school.* Fire erupted in her stomach, climbing through her chest to her cheeks.

Amber dropped her armful on the desk and flopped onto her bed, fully clothed, curling into her pillow. She shook with silent sobs until oblivion claimed her again.

3

OLD HABITS AND ALL THAT

Josh sat on the open tailgate of his truck, rubbing his hands to warm them. He hadn't bothered to stuff gloves into his pockets this morning, but then he hadn't planned on sitting outside for any length of time either. A light dusting of snow covered the green patches around the sparsely filled parking lot and arboretum behind the college. He kept one eye on the white Mini two rows over, and one on the side entrance into the film studies hall. Josh usually parked at the front of the school; he didn't like wasting time. Just in and out and gone. But not today.

Amber had been back for just over a week and Josh still hadn't run into her. He didn't see her around school, different courses and all, but he had paid attention to when her car was in the driveway. As luck had it, she'd left early this morning and he'd caught up to her at the turn-off into the school from the boulevard. Saw where she parked and figured he'd "run into her" there after school.

"This is stupid. What am I doing?" Josh's breath puffed white in the air. He jumped down, fists jammed into his winter jacket, and hunched his shoulders up. An incoming text *cha-chinged*. Payday. As Josh reached for his phone in his back pocket, a voice stopped him.

"Hey, man! What are you doing over here?" his buddy Sanj called. Josh turned and watched as two girls staggered away from Sanj and Jimmy toward the residences. The girls' laughter carried through the crisp air. They waved at the guys then dashed off. Josh grinned as the guys zipped their jackets and hustled over to join him. The greenhouses were notorious for "study breaks".

"Where's Gord?" Josh asked, scanning the area.

Jimmy smirked. "Studying with his tutor." He and Sanj elbowed each other back and forth. They'd been goofs since high school.

"So? Why you here?" Sanj asked, lifting his chin to point at the Lot 1 sign.

"Front was full this morning."

"Bullshit," Jimmy said. "You look like you're waiting for someone."

Josh shrugged. "You guys still planning on Daytona?"

"Hell, yeah." Jimmy stomped his feet. "Bustin' outa this place early, too. Don't want to miss the race, ya know." He waggled his eyebrows.

"Right. Like I'm going to buy that. You just don't want to miss the fun on the beach."

All three laughed.

Sanj punched Josh in the arm. "Come with us, man."

"Nah, can't. Next time. Dad's got me scheduled for work."

"Get a pass, make it up after school's out." Sanj flipped his collar up against a gust.

"I took a pass over Christmas. Gotta do this one. You booked your flights yet?" Josh shifted to look over Jimmy's shoulder as the film studies door swung open. A girl bundled in an oversized white parka fringed in fur and wearing a long blue and silver scarf hustled out. He didn't have to see her face to know who it was. His chest tightened. He tried to swallow past a dry throat then glanced at his friends, his mind reeling. *How the hell do I get them to leave? She won't even look at me if they're around.* He sighed. *Gotta give 'em what they want.*

"Look. You guys gotta scram." He tilted his head toward the walking parka.

"Ooo-hoo, I knew it. Gonna make your move." Jimmy double-fisted the air in front of Josh's gut.

"Come on. Get lost already. I'll tell you about it if it goes anywhere." It wouldn't, and he wouldn't. He just wanted to talk to her. That's all he ever wanted to do after what happened in grade nine; he just hadn't grown a set until now. Josh grabbed the backs of their jackets and pushed his friends toward the closest entrance. They laughed at him, held their hands up in surrender, and took off.

Josh turned back and scanned the lot. The white parka opened the Mini's door. He jogged forward to the next set of cars, but she slipped into her vehicle and shut him out. Again. A stone or maybe his heart plummeted. Everything he'd wanted to say solidified in his throat. He leaned against a dark blue sedan and sucked in air. An alarm blasted at him. Amber pulled out of the lot and Josh hoofed-it back to his truck.

Maybe I can pull in the driveway at the same time. Finally get a chance to talk…

But the thought that spurred him to follow her off campus was not the same one going through his head at the lights.

What the hell are you doing? Following her? That's stalker shit, man.

She drove straight through the signal on Humber College Blvd; he turned right onto HWY 27 knowing the second Amber saw him, she'd make a beeline for the house before he even crossed the street. It had been a stupid idea. He took the right onto Queens Plate Drive and coasted behind the mall.

A black SUV pulled out of the Woodbine Centre's back lot

as Josh passed. It looked kinda familiar. He shrugged off the notion. Black was the third most popular colour; it could be anyone.

But as Josh drove through the lights at Rexdale, heading for the casino, the SUV followed him, racing through the yellow, crowding his bumper. The back of his neck tingled in warning. He rolled his shoulders and turned left onto Grandstand, bypassing the parking lot and heading back out to Rexdale Blvd. Josh made the light before the SUV, and drove home.

Amber's empty car sat in the driveway. He stared at it as he waited on the street for his garage door to open. That needling sensation in his chest returned. Prior to last week, he hadn't seen her in over a year – wasn't sure if he'd ever see her again; and now she was home. Just like that and all those things left unsaid frothed back to the surface.

He pulled into the garage and stared at her car until the automatic door blocked it from sight. Sighing, he hopped out of the truck, grabbed his backpack, and headed inside.

"Okay, thank you," his mom said, hanging up the phone in the kitchen and walking into the living room through the dining room. "They've booked us into the alternate. It should be fine. The refund is minimal for the difference in price so I got them to add it as credit to our room." She sat on the white couch she'd bought from Wayfair last month to replace their old leather couch. This one didn't fart when you sat on it, *being a cotton blend and all*, sang his mother's voice. Josh rolled his eyes and locked the door behind him.

"That's good. Check-in time the same?" Josh's dad asked. He didn't see his father, who likely sat in the matching wingback chair in the corner. Josh decided against grabbing a snack, shoved his coat and runners into the closet, and headed for the stairs.

His father cleared his throat.

Josh's nerves sizzled. He turned, one foot on the stairs,

hand on the railing, and looked at his father's right ear as the man now stood in the entryway. A vice gripped his chest, forcing him to breathe past the clamp.

"Did you transfer the money?" The question was for Josh, not his mother.

"I just got home," Josh said.

"That's not what I asked."

"It came through while I was driving. I'll do it in my room."

His dad crossed his arms. "I can wait."

A hot wave blasted past the grip on his lungs, engulfing Josh's entire body. He swallowed then grabbed his phone from his back pocket and swiped over to his banking app.

"There. It's done." He turned to head up the stairs.

"Your mother and I will be leaving first week of February."

"For how long?" he asked, going two steps higher.

"Two weeks." Josh didn't appreciate the edge to his father's voice – even if he deserved it. He glanced at the empty teak table in the corner of the stairwell and the faint shadow of the marble statue that used to sit there. They hadn't replaced it on purpose.

"Okay then. Gotta study." He didn't, but they didn't need to know that.

His mom's voice filtered up the stairwell and down the hall as he reached his room. "Maybe we should cancel."

Josh didn't wait to hear his father's reply. He'd heard the argument often enough to know she'd relent when he reminded her about how long they'd been planning for this trip.

He pulled his phone out and flopped down onto his bed calling up the Warhammer app to keep him occupied until dinner. Josh also got into Discord, and texted a bet into the gamer-verse.

4

A GODZILLA KIND OF DAY

Amber futzed with her backpack on the floor between her feet. Not all of her books fit along with her lunch. She glanced at the close-circuit monitor mounted to the ceiling of the registrar hallway-turned-waiting room. It read 126 for the past ten minutes; each ticket taking exponentially longer. *Maybe I should've grabbed a number before last class. At this rate I won't have time to eat.* She returned to reorganizing her pack. Squashed sandwiches were not a delicacy.

Number 127 popped up. *Figures. As soon as I get into something it changes.* Amber jammed her books haphazardly back into her bag, stuffing her lunch in her parka pockets instead, and slid from the hard-plastic chair. She walked around the glass partition to speak with the Registrar Rep. He fidgeted with something on his computer and didn't look at her. She dropped her book bag on the floor and he jerked his head up.

"How can I help you?" he asked.

"The Student Advisor wants to see me about my transfer status."

"ID please."

She handed over her student card.

"Please wait over there." He pointed at a break in the long desk. Amber hauled her pack onto her shoulder.

A chic, East-Asian woman with close-cropped, purple-streaked hair approached the dividing line.

She held out her hand. "Amber Martin?"

Amber shook it but the woman's grip barely squeezed her fingers before disappearing again.

"Follow me, please."

Amber nodded and the transfer Advisor led her on a circuitous route through the maze of office partitions. By the time they hit the middle of the labyrinth, Amber forgot the route back.

The petite woman set herself down on a moulded acrylic office chair at an equally plastic desk with metal legs before rotating around. Amber stood behind the minimalist guest chair that matched the stark grey of the desk and every other office she'd caught sight of as they'd passed.

"Please, have a seat. I'm Wendy So." She leaned forward with her hands clasped.

Amber sat and shifted her pack down between her feet.

"Thank you for coming. I'm sorry this has taken so long. With the start of any semester it always takes several weeks for us to get caught up with requests."

Two weeks to verify what Amber already knew was insane. But the college held the hoops and so she had to jump.

Wendy tilted one of the monitors to face Amber, typed something, and highlighted sections appeared on the screen.

"These are your records from Fanshawe, specifically the electives in question. We have accepted all of your Broadcasting Journalism grades but we don't have an equivalent for the Children's Theatre and Puppetry Arts elective you took last semester."

Amber's chest tightened. *This isn't happening.* The Media Studies Chair at Humber and the Dean at Fanshaw had both assured her there'd be no issues with the transfer. Her already overfull schedule meant spare-time equalled pipe-dreams.

"I don't understand. Dean Richards said there wouldn't be a problem."

"And there isn't. All of your core courses have been transferred along with the respective grades. You will, however, need to take another elective before you graduate next year. The options for evening and summer courses are quite varied. I'm sure you'll have no problem selecting something that appeals to you and meets the criteria for the diploma."

The sanity locked inside Amber shattered. Tired of dealing with school politics, she barely managed an even breath before responding. "But I don't have the time or the money to take an extra course. I was assured this wouldn't be an issue." *I need this resolved, yesterday.* "Look, is there some kind of appeal process?" Amber glanced at the clock on the bottom of the monitor – five minutes before her Radio II course started, and it was on the far side of campus.

"That's highly irregular," Ms. So said.

"But possible."

"Yes, I suppose. You'd have to speak with several course directors to gain approval for an equivalent credit and–"

"Can you email the process to me as well as this"–Amber waved at the computer screen–"assessment? I can't afford to be late for class." She stood up and hugged her pack in an effort to calm her rapid heartrate. *This isn't supposed to be an issue. It's bad enough I gave up my scholarship to come here. Now I have to run around looking for someone who knows absolutely nothing about me to back me on this?*

"Well, yes. I suppose. You know I can give you a late-access slip, right? You don't need to rush."

"You've obviously never met Professor Van Dorn. Thank you, but no. An email." Amber's gaze flicked to the time again. She turned and supressed a scream. It was bad enough she had to move back home, but between her dad and her workload, the last thing she needed was to take yet another course *or* be late for this stupid class.

Amber scrambled out of the partitioned office that had no door, locked her gaze onto the bulkhead denoting the main reception desk, and fumbled along the narrow aisles until the labyrinth spat her out. She raced from the soaring ceilings of the new wing, up the ramp, and around the corner into the cave-like original building. Her usual route of crossing the courtyard and skirting around the crammed halls was not an option. But, as much of a hurry as she was in, Amber hesitated drawing closer to the lounge opposite the Bookstore.

Most of the kids from West Humber Collegiate ended up attending Humber College, and she didn't need that kind of attention. She wasn't there to relive her abysmal high school dramas. Still, it was class change. She could blend in. Disappear.

Attaching herself to a random group of students headed in her general direction, she merged with the crowd. They ambled on, chatting as if the world wasn't going to end if they didn't get to their next class. *Ugh! Too slow. Forget this.* Amber maneuvered around them, dodging the oncoming walkers as she wove her way to the upper ramp.

A blonde with rainbow highlights plunked down in the lounge and met Amber's gaze. The girl smiled and wiggled her fingers. Amber smiled back. Tonya lived just up Kearney Drive from her. They'd never been besties, but she'd also never insulted Amber, so that put her in the good books – one of only a handful of people from that school who hadn't listened to the rumours.

The crowd thinned ten feet before the ramp. Amber's skin prickled. With her peripheral vision, she scanned the lounge on her left and then the Java Jazz café on her right.

Oh, shit.

He sat there in his leather school jacket with a leg dangling over the back of the mint-green seat, surrounded by his usual cronies. Josh's piercing eyes stared at her. She caught the cadence of his voice and snatches of the conversation as he boasted:

"My dad wants me managing the north Cineplex so he can buy out..." But he stopped talking, which only made his gang look around to see what caught his eye.

Heat rushed from Amber's neck into her cheeks as she forced her gaze forward. Her heart leaped into her throat and her ears burned. She crashed into someone walking the opposite way and tried to steady herself without losing any books from her over-stuffed bag. Amber hugged the pack to her chest, stutter-stepping.

Laughter echoed in the expansive hallway. Josh separated himself from the others, waving them off as he jogged over. Amber didn't need to know what might be going through *his* mind – what gossip still clung to her because of his asinine comments five and a half years ago. But something in the way he looked at her reminded Amber of the sweet boy who'd tripped over his words asking her out. Her skin flashed from fire to ice and back again. She shook her head.

I don't belong here. If it weren't for–

But she didn't want to think about that. She sighed and ran up the raised corridor to her class. The closed door made her heart dislodge from her throat and drop into her shoes. Amber twisted the knob and opened the door. Her instructor stopped mid-sentence and the entire class turned to look at her.

———

Amber grabbed the lid from the noodle pot and dropped it.

"Ow!" She blew on tender fingers and pulled an oven mitt out of the drawer. The cheese gooed nicely and blended with the rigatoni. She slopped in half a can of tomato-basil soup and stirred until the sauce turned pink – a favourite of her roomies back at Fanshawe.

The front door banged open and a blast of frosty air whipped into the hot kitchen. Amber pulled the breaded chicken out of the oven, setting the tray on the back burner.

"You're just in time," she called over her shoulder.

"I can't stay. Just dropping off my briefcase," her dad called back.

Amber hustled across the kitchen and over to the door. She jammed her padded fists on her hips. "Bullshit. Take your boots off and come sit down."

"Your mother–"

"Knows you'll be there soon. *And* she knows you need to eat. No more last-minute midnight meals, Dad. You've had two weeks to adjust to me being back. I'm not here to enable you. I'm here to keep you healthy. *I expect you at the table in five minutes.*" She gave an internal start – those were her mother's words. Amber bit her lip and pushed back a wave of emotion, blinking back unwanted tears.

He frowned at her and pressed his lips together in a fine line. She took a breath. Maybe swearing had been a bit overboard, but she'd gotten his attention. Amber didn't wait for a reply. She went back into the kitchen and served dinner.

Exactly five minutes later her dad returned from washing up and sat down at the table across from her. Neither of them said a word. In high school he would've asked about her day. She was glad he didn't. But the slight crease marring his forehead said he did have something on his mind. They avoided looking at Mom's empty place setting. Amber knew he had more to say than she wanted to hear, so she didn't ask him about his day either. Besides, it wasn't anything she hadn't heard before...

"Amber Martin, please come down to the office. Amber Martin, to the office," the school's secretary blasted over the intercom during

lunch. Of course, every person in the café watched as she scraped her chair back from an empty table.

Dad waited outside the main office, foot tapping, looking around trying to spot her. When he did his frown deepened. Amber's gut tightened and the hand gripping her backpack spasmed.

"I've signed you out. Let's go."

"What are you talking about? I have a test this afternoon. What's going on?"

He just gave her that look; the same one he wore since grade eight when Mom first got diagnosed; the same one Amber saw every time she was told they didn't have the money to do something because Mom's meds came first.

Dad walked past. She followed, like always. Now Mr. Burke would have to put together a different test just for her and every pair of eyes in math class would silently curse Amber for getting one more night to study. Pictures of chain-sawed logs would get posted on her locker and shoved into the vents in retaliation for something she had no control over.

Amber fumed the whole way to the hospital.

Her body quaked between being scared and being angry.

As the doctor spoke with Dad, she made herself walk past them and over to Mom's room. Amber caught the doctor saying something about Mom needing someone to watch her for the next few days; not being able to stay in the hospital; just a precaution but necessary.

Amber let her anger win.

She heard herself say things she'd never put into words before, never wanted to believe were true. And like a riptide, it submersed and carried her over the falls.

"No! I won't do it. How am I supposed to graduate in three months if you keep pulling me out of school for babysitting duty? I have a major test this afternoon. A trip to the Science Centre tomorrow that's crucial for my final project that I've already paid for from my own money. My life is constantly being put on hold because of you and it's not fair! What am I going to be left with *when you're gone, huh? I'll be working for minimum wage trying to get my GED or struggling through night school with Dad working twenty-four seven to get out of debt and no mother."*

She sensed her father and the doctor crowd the doorway. The look on Mom's face broke Amber.

"I know you're dying," I whispered, voice hoarse. "We all know you're dying, but I can't keep putting my life on hold waiting for that to happen."

She turned and pushed her way out, running down the hall, down the street, and away...

Amber had trouble swallowing. She hadn't been alone in a room with her mother in two years.

She and her father ate in relative silence. When he set his knife and fork on an empty plate, Amber stood and cleared the table. She dug around the cupboard under the sink for the dish soap, forgetting she'd rested the oven mitts against the bottle. No unrinsed mounds of dishes littered the counter or stove anymore. If her Dad grabbed a late-night snack after getting in, he made sure to scrub up, now.

Amber reached for the faucet.

"She wants to see you," he said.

Her hand, hovering over the tap, twitched.

"I told her you left the scholarship." He sighed but still hadn't risen to get ready. Her dad had been in such a hurry to leave before even steeping foot in the door, and now... now, that driving burn had fizzled out. Now, he was a man trying to do too much. A familiar ache resonated in her chest, but she didn't turn around. Amber knew if she looked at him, she'd break her resolve. She'd let fear win.

"I called her yesterday. She never said anything. Never said you told her."

"I didn't. She guessed it. Talked about how the colour had returned to my cheeks. That I must be eating better. She's smart, your mother. I didn't have to tell her. Come with me tonight."

The dark abyss yawned, threatening to overwhelm Amber as icy spikes of dread engulfed her. She couldn't think of how much time she'd lost since that outburst; how much she relied on the distance as a cushion from the truth.

"I can't. I have a paper due tomorrow and I don't want to be up after midnight working on it. Tell her I say, hi. I'll call her on the weekend." She turned the water on and filled the sink with dishes. By the time Amber got to scrapping leftovers into storage containers, she risked a glance over her shoulder. He was gone.

The door scraped shut. She closed her eyes and took a deep breath, holding it until her lungs burned. She released the air and then carried on with tidying up, forcing her brain to ignore what the Student Advisor had said; ignore walking into class late; ignore the laugh track that followed her from high school; and definitely ignore the boy across the street who started it all. But mostly, ignore the fact her mother lay dying in the hospital.

5

FOR PETE'S SAKE

As Amber kicked open the front door, her keys dropped onto the mat. Nudging them with her boot, she pushed them into the foyer while clutching two rather large totes of groceries, shifting her book bag higher onto her back. She used her knee to shut the door and lugged everything into the kitchen.

With still no word about her appeal after two more weeks of waiting, she'd registered for a HUMA course: Popular Culture ~ An Interdisciplinary Perspective. Amber didn't need another class overviewing today's world in art, but according to Humber, she did if she wanted to graduate. It ran until 6:00 p.m. but she had still needed to pick up a few things for meals after school – something her dad could have easily done on the weekend, but Amber knew he'd be at the hospital all day, each day. After being home for six weeks, she knew the routine well.

As Amber restocked the cupboards and fridge, she mulled over an idea for her magazine class. She hated what was going on with the government and Indigenous people these days. The lack of funding to help them and the argument about land rights made her angry – they deserved better. But she wasn't an activist, she was an artist; a writer. Her dad always said, *find a way to help someone help themselves and you both just might learn something.*

If her magazine celebrated Indigenous cultures and the First Nations peoples, gave them a viable outlet to advertise and sell their craft, then she might be able to take a basic online periodical and turn it into *Women's World* for Natives. In fact, she remembered reading an article in newspaper class about a group of Chippewa girls already trying to do just that, but not having the backing they needed. If she reached out–

"Damnit."

She pushed the tote bags around the kitchen floor with her foot. *Forgot milk.* Amber leaned against the counter with outstretched hands and let her head hang toward her chest. Just one more thing she had to try and fit into an already busy night. She cursed again and pushed off, dragging herself back to the front hall. Yanking on her damp boots, she shrugged her jacket on and snatched the keys from the floor. The light her dad had on a timer already shone, a dull glow.

Back in the Mini, she yanked her driving gloves on and thanked the powers that be that reading week started on Monday. She needed a break. Amber headed for the convenience store just up the way. She was supposed to be going to a ski lodge with Kim and Nanci, but that fell through when she decided to move back home. Still, vegging out in the basement rec room was better than playing hide and seek with the crowd at school. Warmer, too, on both accounts.

As Amber turned onto Mercury Road, her lights glanced over a silver truck half-on, half-off the road on the opposite side of the street – at the walkway to the river. The driver's door hung wide open and a blue dash light blinked.

What's going on?

She pulled over just past the vehicle and tossed the Mini

into park. She looked around, twisting this way and that to see behind her and off to the side.

No one.

Nothing.

Her stomach clenched, but not in fear. Nothing crazy ever happened in her neighbourhood. It was an older subdivision with a lot of young families and retired couples.

Worry compelled her to snatch her phone and check it out. She didn't want to call 911 and have it be some drunk taking a piss in Mrs. Randall's bushes. He'd be gone before they arrived. And if that was the case, it was probably Yellena's Great Uncle. Amber's old babysitter always had strange stories about her extended family. Amber clicked on her phone light as she walked past the truck and beyond the streetlamp onto the shadowed path.

She tracked her beam back and forth over the frost-tipped grass. The black cloak of the bushes guarded the way to the river and gave her the creeps.

Maybe I should just leave it alone.

Then her beam caught a flash of red just down the trail. Her heart jumped. She trained the light back on the bright splotch and just stood there, squinting, trying to decipher what her eyes were telling her.

"Holy shit."

A body.

She nearly dropped her phone trying to dial the police. A ragged cough broke the quiet as air rasped down someone's throat. The shoe attached to the leg, attached to the red jacket, shifted. Amber didn't finish dialing. She ran to the person whose cough turned into a groan. She dropped down beside them.

"Hey, are you okay?" She reached out to touch the coat. Another moan and the person rolled onto his back. Her hand hovered as his swollen and bloodied face came into view.

Josh.

"What the hell? Josh. Josh, can you hear me?" Amber dropped her phone and reached with both hands to hold his face, but didn't. She didn't want to hurt him more, even if he deserved it. He licked his lips.

"Caber?" he forced the word past a fat lip and dry throat. Amber shoved his shoulder.

"I told you not to call me that, asshole."

He tried to crack a smile, but his heavily swollen eye told her that wasn't the only bruising he faced; he coughed again, wincing. "Need. Help."

"Forget that. I'll call your folks." She snatched up her cell, ready to punch in their number. She'd deleted it from her contact list two phones ago, but she remembered it just fine.

"Va–Vacation," he sputtered, cringing and curling in on himself, shuddering.

"Then I'll get Jimmy or Gordon or Sanj."

"Gone," he choked out.

"Left for break early? Why am I not surprised. Cheaper flights?"

He didn't answer. In fact, he'd grown awfully still. A tightness gripped her chest. She leaned forward. His breath played across the bridge of her nose. He didn't smell of alcohol, just his usual minty-Altoid pig-headed self. Amber sat up.

"Then I'll call the cops."

His one good eye sprang open and he grabbed her arm in a vice grip. "No." He struggled for breath.

"Look at you. Whoever gave you this beatdown might have broken your ribs. You need medical attention."

He didn't speak again but the sheer terror in his eyes said everything. Amber desperately wanted to leave him there. After everything he'd put her through it was the least he deserved. But the last thing she needed was his death on her conscience. Josh didn't deserve that much real estate in her mind. He already took up too much as it was.

"Oh, fine. Come on, then." Amber twisted her wrist within his grip, held onto as much of his forearm as she could, and pulled. He rolled onto his knees and staggered to his feet. Josh bent nearly in two. He gasped short shuddering breaths that travelled from his arm and hand into hers. Amber frowned and shoved down the ever-present anger in order to listen to her compassion. She hadn't always hated him. He was in pain and she only made it worse.

"Where are your keys?" Amber asked.

He attempted to wave his free arm.

"I don't understand."

"Bushes," he forced out. His normally sturdy frame quaked in her arms. He'd never been this fragile. Common sense chipped away at her shell. He wasn't going to last on his feet much longer.

They hobbled together along the path to the street and bypassed his truck. Amber did her best not to dump him in the passenger seat of her car, but the small vehicle didn't make for ease of maneuvering. He bumped his head on the doorframe, cringed, then sunk into the space. For some reason, now that he was no longer in her arms, her heartrate doubled and her anxiety rose.

He wasn't faking it.

Josh was really hurt.

Amber launched into the driver's seat and peeled away with a U-ie, heading back down their street. But she couldn't take him home. He probably had a concussion and she couldn't risk leaving him alone. With his cronies out of town and his insistence not to get the authorities involved, she really had only one option left. Her gut twisted as her mind replayed that Monday morning at school after their third week dating, back in grade nine. He didn't deserve her sympathy. He didn't deserve jack-all.

She pulled into her driveway, unlocked the front door, and hurried to extricate her ex-boyfriend from the confines of the car. They stumbled into the house and down to the rec room. Amber's legs wavered under his unsupported weight. She tumbled onto the couch with him, a tangle of arms and legs – exactly the opposite of what he'd accused her of all those years ago.

But he didn't try anything. In fact, he barely moved. She slipped off his battered body, even as her own remembered the nearness far more keenly than she thought possible. Amber shook herself, knelt on the floor, and leaned over him.

"Josh. Wake up. You can't fall asleep. Wake up, I said." She used her "go screw-yourself" tone and he cracked open his good eye. "I'm guessing I should rescue your truck next?"

He gave a weak smile and a slight chin lift for confirmation.

"Then you've gotta promise me you'll still be awake when I get back."

He closed his eye and nodded. His usual tan complexion verged on grey. Amber raided the chest freezer and returned with two bags of frozen veggies. Josh jolted when she angled one over his eye and swollen lip, the other over his ankle – apparently one of the many reasons he had trouble walking. She left him in his coat but removed his boots and shoved them in the laundry tub on her way back up the stairs. Amber didn't even lock the door on her way out. Her feet picked up more and more speed until she ran full-tilt down Kearney Street.

The cold air sliced at her throat and chilled her from the inside out, wicking the heat from her cheeks and the thoughts from her mind. Amber panted as she stumbled to a stop against Josh's truck just around the corner on Mercury. Turning on her phone light again, she searched the bushes he'd tried to point out earlier. She trained the beam on the top of the short shrub and leaned close to the branches, tilting her screen from side to side to help her look into every nook and cranny. But, now that she wasn't running, her thoughts caught up with her.

What the hell happened to him? Who would have done this? Why would he have gotten out of his truck, let alone felt the need to chuck his keys? What have I gotten myself into? He doesn't deserve my help. When I get home, we're figuring out who he can stay with because it sure as hell isn't going to be me.

Finally, at the base of the shrubs tucked back against the main trunk, a metallic glint caught her eye. Braving a few sharp jabs and scratches, she snatched up the keys just as a strange grumbling motor crawled toward the truck from the main road. Amber shut off the light on her phone and hid behind the prickly evergreen bush, watching a black El Camino low-rider creep into the pool of the streetlight as it rumbled past Josh's truck. She thought it stopped at one point, but couldn't be sure since it disappeared on the other side of the silver vehicle. That, and a number of pine boughs, blocked her view.

Her body shook, and not from the cold. She tried to swallow past the growing lump in her throat. "I'm gonna kill you," she whispered, shivering, and waited another ten minutes before hauling ass to Josh's truck, slamming the door, and driving off.

6

BROKEN PIECES

Amber managed to close the front door without banging it, taking the time to hang up her coat and tuck her boots away. She spared half a glance at the kitchen as she passed on her way to the rec room stairs. Dinner would have to wait. Didn't have milk anyway, so she'd have to make something else. But really, Amber clung to thoughts of dinner only to keep away thoughts of what just happened.

At the bottom of the stairs she stopped short. Across the room, past the air hockey table and the old pinball machines, her four-year nightmare lay beaten and bruised. She wanted to feel self-satisfied and righteous that the ass-hat finally got what he deserved, but even in her darkest moments she never wished *this* on him, or anyone else for that matter. He was a prick, yes, and an asshole, but not a monster – not really. It was monsters who did this to him.

His chest rose and fell, calm and even. At first her relief loosened the tense muscles in her neck, but then–

"Josh. Josh wake up." Her heart grew spikes. She ran over and dropped down beside him. Her hands hovered inches away from his chest ready to shake him. *He might have a fractured rib or severe bruising.* She held back. He cracked open his good eye.

"You cursing me?" He lifted the corner of his mouth not hidden by the bag of frozen peas.

She squinted at him, and shoved him anyway. He coughed and pulled his knees up for protection.

"Jackass." Amber brought her hands up again, and he flinched. "Don't be such a baby. Let me look at the damage." He uncurled enough to give her access. She lifted the peas off his face. Her brow furrowed and she pursed her lips.

"That bad, huh?" He coughed and winced.

She met his gaze for a moment, then looked back at the split in his lip and the goose-egg distorting his eye. Other bruises reddened his jaw, and blood from his nose dried on his upper lip and shirt. Amber grabbed her phone and searched for: *signs of a concussion.*

"How do you feel?" she asked.

"Like shit."

"That doesn't help. Do you have a headache?" She glanced up from the list populating her screen.

"If I said no, would you believe me?"

"No."

"Then don't ask."

"Okay, fair enough. What about your vision? Are you seeing spots? Stars? Is anything foggy or hazy?"

His good eye rotated in its socket, doing ocular calisthenics. "No. I saw spots when they were hitting me but not since you showed up."

"Are you dizzy? Do you feel like you're going to hurl?"

He sat up with a grimace and a sharp breath. "No. I mean, I don't feel great but I'm not at risk of bringing anything up."

"Well, you're talking fine and answering without hesitation. Is there a ringing in your ears? Are you tired?"

"Stop it."

"What?"

"I'm fine."

"The hell you are." She put her phone to sleep and slipped it back into her pocket. "What the happened to you? I went back to get your truck and I swear someone drove by casing the place. I ought to call the cops and be done with you. Drop you off in emerg and let the professionals–"

"Don't." A wavering fear shook the firmness from his voice. "I pissed someone off. They won't be back." He struggled to stand up. "Just take me home, Caber."

"It's Amber, you shithead. You call me that one more time and I'll break another rib." She shoved him back onto the couch. "Stay there. I need to clean you up. If you won't go to the cops or let me call an ambulance, I'll have to make sure you don't die tonight sleeping with a concussion."

"I don't have a concussion."

She stormed off, ignoring him, and found the first aid kit in the laundry room. The connotations to *tossing dead wood* had followed her around high school far too long. Caber Tossing became synonymous with Amber Miller, and how Josh had up-ended and tossed her aside after nearly two months for being wooden. The second she didn't have to worry about him dying, he'd be out on his ass in the street. Him being there just complicated issues she'd clarified for herself long ago.

Amber grabbed a couple of rags and ran warm water into the puke bucket. It was a normal enough pail, but her mother preferred to Swiffer everything these days – or had – and the only reason anyone took the bucket out was when they were sick.

She arranged her supplies on the floor, tossed a throw pillow from the recliner onto the carpet, and knelt down by Josh again. This time, he stared at the ceiling, the smirk gone.

"I'm sorry," he said. But she didn't let him finish. She didn't need excuses.

"Here, take these. They should help with the pain." She

placed two extra strength Advil on his palm and rested the guest cup from the downstairs bathroom against his tender lips, dribbling a bit of cool water into his mouth. Some of it trickled down the side of his chin but she caught it with her fingers, rasping against a day's worth of beard growth. He downed the meds as she wrung out the damp rag, drips punctuating the air like a storm crossing the Humber River. But she left enough moisture in the cloth to help loosen the dried blood without scrubbing his face raw.

Amber leaned forward, her hair cascading around his face. Her locket slipped forward and swung above Josh's nose. She tucked it back into her shirt. He closed his eye.

"Hang on." Amber draped the cloth over the edge of the bucket and retrieved an elastic from her back pocket. After tying her hair up, she resumed. Josh kept his eye closed as she gingerly worked on removing the blood.

Amber traced around his nose, trying not to bump it. It didn't look broken, but someone had certainly punched him a good one. She lifted the frozen veggies and daubed around his inflated eye, following the trail of blood down the side of his face to his ear and neck.

As she worked, she focused on her task and not him. In grade nine, she'd fallen for his dark, Mediterranean looks: the long lashes and thick, wavy black hair. He'd said the green eyes came from his great grandmother. But the luck of the Irish hadn't done anything from stopping the train-wreck that had been their relationship. Well, the seven weeks they'd dated had been perfect; what came after destroyed her.

Amber dropped the cloth into the reddened water and used the other rag to pat his face and neck dry. The split lip and slice beside his swollen eye still needed attention. She rummaged around in the kit and pulled out the Detol. The acrid stench of the sanitizer made her nauseous, but she poured a bunch onto a gauze pad, recapped the bottle, and moved closer to the couch to administer the treatment.

"That stuff reeks," Josh muttered.

"You don't want your cuts to get infected. Lay still." She swooped in and put the cleanser on the slice by his eye.

"OW!" He bucked. She pressed harder to keep the gauze from falling off. Pain flickered in his eye and he fell back to the couch. Still. Silent.

Amber removed the pad. "Josh?"

Nothing.

She nudged his shoulder with the back of her hand. "Josh."

Still nothing.

"Josh! That's not funny."

But he didn't crack a smile. He didn't move. She looked at his chest and couldn't tell if he was breathing. "Oh, shit. What have I done?"

Amber leaned forward and placed her ear near his mouth. She couldn't hear anything, couldn't feel any air. Her ribs squeezed her lungs. She gasped short breaths searching his body for any sign of life, then dropped her head to his chest and placed her ear over it. Her own rapid heart pumped too much blood. She had to take deep steadying breaths to calm down enough to hear properly.

There it was. A slow steady beat.

She lay there a moment longer just listening and letting the rhythm of his heart settle her own, something she'd done only one other time–

"Amber? You home?" Her dad's voice carried as if from far away. She jolted to her feet, adrenaline spiking, and looked at the clock on the DVR under the TV.

"Coming!" She nabbed the frozen veggie bags, slipped back into the laundry room, tossed them into the freezer, and pulled out a frozen stir fry pack before jogging up the stairs. Every nerve ending sizzled as her heart did a rapid tango, spinning around in her chest.

"Hey, Dad." She sucked in a deep breath. "Lost track of

time. Got a couple of assignments due Friday before the break. Something simple tonight?" She held up the large bag of frozen food. He eyed it and then the kitchen. Amber was certain he'd wave it off and go eat at the hospital. But he didn't. He took the bag and waved her off instead.

"Get back to work. I'll make dinner."

A mix of joy and fear rushed through her veins. Amber desperately wanted to go downstairs and monitor Josh. She'd knocked him out with that spike of pain, and now that he was unconscious she needed to be there. On the other hand, she hadn't lied about the projects and here was her dad doing 'dad stuff' and making an effort to help her out, instead of racing off to the hospital again.

Amber popped up onto her toes and gave him a kiss on the cheek. "Thanks, Dad. Call me when it's ready." She couldn't risk heading back down to the rec room with him home. If he found Josh, he'd get the authorities involved. So Amber forced her feet to carry her down the hall to sit in the middle of her bed with her work spread out around her.

She didn't read anything.

She didn't write anything.

She sat there listening to her father putter in the kitchen as she worried about the boy in her basement who might stop breathing. The fact her mother might also stop breathing wasn't the same. She'd been 'dying' for a long time now.

7

CURB-SIDE PHILOSOPHY

Two days later, Amber yawned, and snapped a banana off the bunch hanging from the holder on the counter and set it on the small plate beside the toast with peanut butter. The darkness outside had a light quality to it as the sun edged up over the horizon. She clicked off the kitchen radio in the middle of the unseasonably warm forecast they'd predicted for the week. It had been another long night, but she was fairly certain between her assignments and Josh they were all on the right track.

Amber grabbed the glass of OJ off the table and headed for the stairs, nudging the door open with her toes. She crept down just in case he hadn't woken up yet. Yesterday, she'd ended up leaving both his breakfast and dinner sitting on the end table by the couch. The swelling in his ankle and around his lips and eye had finally gone down, but the purple bruises turned greeny-yellow giving a gangrenous hue to his olive skin.

Amber turned at the bottom of the stairs and stopped short.

Joshua Patrick Bianchi, what the hell are you doing! But the words stuck in her throat as she stared at the would-be invalid, foot up on a cushion on the coffee table playing Mario Cart on her old Wii.

"Yes! Champion of the Mushroom Cup. Still number one." He raised his hands and the wheel-shaped controller into the air making a roaring-crowd sound.

Amber shifted, not sure why she was bringing breakfast to someone who could clearly take care of himself.

"Caber! Food. I'm starving–" His eyes lost their sparkle and his smile dropped. "*Amber...* I didn't mean it. I, it slipped. Too used to–"

Amber slammed the dishes onto the air hockey table and jammed her fists onto her hips.

"Get out!" She pointed to the stairs.

"I didn't mean–I mean, I didn't–Shit."

"Get out! I don't believe you!" She stomped into the laundry room and chucked one boot after another at him. He hopped on one foot while yanking his jacket over his arms, wincing. Josh caught his first boot but the second one hit him in the chest. Amber chased him around the coffee table.

"After everything I did for you, you lounge around here like I'm your personal goddamn maid and call me names."

She harassed him up the stairs.

"You're lucky I'm not a sadist and didn't just leave you out there or called the cops like I should have."

He yanked the front door open.

"Get the hell out of my house and don't come back!" Amber slammed it shut, her entire body vibrating with furry. She should have known better.

Amber sucked in air and held it in her lungs all the way back downstairs. When she picked up the breakfast from the air hockey table, she slowly let the breath out all the way back to the kitchen. After downing the OJ, she tossed the toast into the bio-bin under the sink and set the banana on the counter under the bunch. Grabbing her backpack, she left for school.

"I KNOW I promised not to assign anything other than reading for next week, but I feel a reminder about your magazine proposals is necessary based on the questions many of you have been asking this week. And so, bearing that in mind, I'm releasing you to your own devices an hour early. Have a good break." Professor Umi smiled and shooed everyone out of the room.

Amber didn't bother to put her coat on as she shuffled into the corridor. She headed for Parking Lot 1, past the area for Film Studies, toward the Arboretum. A warm breeze caressed her cheeks and made her second-guess wearing a t-shirt under her Humber sweater. This year, the mid-winter break just happened to coincide with the mid-winter thaw. *So much for getting some skiing in.* Not that she'd have had the time anyway, but it was nice to pretend.

Amber popped into the Mini and dumped her book bag on the seat beside her. For once, the grey afternoon light shone bright enough that she didn't need to put her headlights on. In fact, she turned the heat off in the car and put her window down for the short drive home.

Only, her brain's autopilot setting didn't drive her home. She found herself parked at the strip mall across from the hospital, again, staring at the cars and ambulances coming and going.

Time had no meaning.

She just stared and stared – transfixed – her mind jumping between arguments about coping with her mother's health and limitations, and absolutely nothing: a frozen mind, a static image, a lost word. Amber knew she should go in; owed it to her mother, to herself after what had happened. They hadn't talked properly since before her stupid outburst. Still...at Fanshawe she'd been able to live her own life, discover things about herself she never knew before. Had it come at too high a price?

Something dripped onto her lap. She blinked and wiped at her face, confused. *Why am I crying?*

Her phone pinged with a text. She glanced at the preview of the message then tossed the device back onto the passenger seat. Mom wanted to know what her plans were for the break. The old wall shot up. She tried to swallow, pushing the bubble in her throat down. With shaky hands, Amber put the car in gear and drove home.

She mauled and squeezed the spike of growing fear into a tiny ball and shoved it as far down inside her as it could go... it was getting crowded down there. *Dad said there's been no change in her condition, so it's not like this is my last chance. She's just trying to coax me to come because I'm around.* Amber wasn't ready to admit to how many times she nearly walked through the hospital doors.

She frowned. Amber had been preparing herself for the inevitability of her mother's death for years. Everything had revolved around what was best for mother at all times, even when she'd claimed to put Amber first. And then, the moment Amber did put herself first, like with the scholarship, she was a horrible person. The blow-up hadn't helped...

Oh, Mom... Her chest tightened; she took in a shuddered breath and held it until the trembles stopped. Amber didn't want her mom to die, but she also couldn't put her life on hold waiting for it to happen.

Movement in the driveway across from her house drew Amber out of her daze. No one was supposed to be around this time of day. She squinted into the rear-view mirror as she pulled up before her garage. The suited men disappeared into a vehicle. A black vehicle. Not a low-rider but an SUV. Still, the distinction didn't settle her already riled stomach.

A dozen butterflies burst from her gut and fluttered around in her chest. Amber gripped the armrest just below the door latch and shifted her gaze from the rear-view to the side mirror. The vehicle slowly backed out of Josh's driveway.

Amber popped the catch, grabbed her pack, coat, and phone, and shoved open the door. Stepping out onto the drive, she shivered and not from the air. Amber shouldered her bag and hip-checked the car door shut before heading up to the house. Her grip tightened on the strap as she fumbled for the house key and dropped the lot onto the porch. Amber bent to retrieve them and risked a glance across the street before standing up again. The SUV pulled out of the driveway and sped off.

It would have been easy to ignore everything, tumble into the house, dive under a pile of blankets, and watch reruns of Big Bang Theory until she forgot about the strange men and Josh; except, his front door hung open. Amber hadn't seen Josh at school today after kicking him out this morning. But then, it would have been weird if she had. With the better weather, she'd taken her usual circuitous route around the lounge and avoided eating lunch in the Student Centre. *Maybe I should call the cops?* But she had no idea who those people were or why the door wasn't shut. Josh's terrified look from the other night flashed in her mind. Something wasn't right.

She dropped her stuff in the foyer, claimed her keys, left, and locked the door behind her. Down at the sidewalk she looked to either side of the street.

Nothing stirred.

No cars.

No people.

Everyone was still at work watching the clock for the last hour before release. Amber tugged on the hem of her sweater and then charged across the street and up Josh's driveway. His truck wasn't out front, but that didn't mean anything. The Bianchi's had a two-car garage.

Amber climbed onto the porch and popped her head around the frame of the front door.

"J–" The word caught in her throat. The place was trashed. A shot of adrenaline launched her across the threshold.

"Josh! Josh!" She stumbled over the Persian area rug half-rolled up, and smashed her shin into a sideways kitchen chair. "Josh! Goddamn you! Say something! Where are you hiding? What's going on–" Amber yanked open the unlatched basement door and gripped the frame to stop from tumbling headlong down the steep steps. Her gaze shot to the corner-landing half-way down, and the heap of arms and legs at odd angles.

Her heart shot up into her throat. She coughed. Stumbling down the steps she tried to push air into her lungs, one sharp breath after the next. Crouched on the last step before the landing, Amber reached a hesitant hand forward.

He groaned.

She grabbed his arm and squeezed. "Josh. Josh answer me. Is anything broken? Are you all right?" At the catch in her voice he opened his eyes and slowly unwound his crumpled form.

"Are they gone?" he rasped running a shaky hand over his face and up through his hair.

"Yes. What happened? What's going on?"

He shook his head and tried to stand but his sore ankle wouldn't support his weight. Amber slipped under his arm, grabbed him around the waist, and helped him up the stairs. The mess in the kitchen must not have registered, but at the threshold to the living and dining room he stopped short.

"No. Oh, God, no, no, no, no, no." He sagged against the wall and closed his eyes. "They took everything."

"Nearly. You have to call the police. You have to call your folks. You have to–"

"No."

"What?" She pulled away and crossed her arms, letting

the wall have him. "Do I need to smack you? Look at this place. Look at you!" She flung her arm up, fingers spread wide before hugging herself. She turned and really took a moment to assess the damage.

"I owe them money." He swallowed. His lips parted with a soft click but closed again.

Amber turned back, glaring. Waiting for more.

"I borrowed a lot of money. Not at first, but over time. I had an in on a horse…"

Amber's eyes widened and then her surprise morphed into a frown. "The track." It wasn't a question. "Casino Woodbine? Horse racing? That's what this is about? Gambling? Are you serious?" She tried to form more words but no sound escaped. Amber looked to the ceiling as if talking to God, but her thoughts were meant more for the cosmos than a single deity. Her knees wobbled and she fell into the over-stuffed lounger, still staring at the ceiling.

"Why haven't you asked your parents to bail you out?" Her dead-pan voice stiffened his spine and shocked her, too.

"I had it under control."

"Obviously not. Call them."

"I can't."

She glared at him. "Why the hell not? You want to be dead before they get home?"

He swallowed. "It's the cruise they're on – where they're staying. Something about 'disconnecting' and whatever. I can't reach them."

"Your grandparents?"

He narrowed his eyes, "Oma's dead and Dad's got signatory rights over Opa's accounts. He's got dementia."

"Sorry. It's been a while." Five and half years to be exact. She knew his other grandparents lived in Italy and didn't speak English. Amber waved a half-hearted arm at the room. "Will this cover it? Your debt? Are they done?"

"No."

She frowned again.

He sighed and slid down the wall to the hardwood floor and leaned an arm on the rolled-up rug. "I'm overdue on my payments. Dad gave me a raise in anticipation of taking over as night manager at the Colossus Cineplex but my paycheque is still smaller during school than it is in the summer. I've been setting aside money. I thought if I took what I had, I could double it at the video poker tables. And that worked. All I had to do was repeat it. Do it again. And I did. I almost had what I needed to pay them back until…"

"Until you lost it all. And now you not only owe them money but you owe them, what? Interest?"

"Yeah. This would be them covering the interest," he said and then shook his head.

"Why are they trying to kill you if you owe them money? Wouldn't it be better to have you in good shape so you can eventually pay them back?"

"Have you never seen the movie Goodfellas or even The Whole Nine Yards? They're done asking nicely. Now, if I want to avoid living in a wheelchair for the rest of my life, I need to settle my debt."

"When?"

"Huh?"

"How long do you have?"

He shrugged. "Five days – maybe. They said something about a week when they gave me that beat down a couple of days ago."

"Hmm…" Amber freed her phone from her back pocket and called up Google.

"What? What are you doing?"

"Selling your truck."

"Excuse me? I don't think so."

"Excuse me, but I do. Look. You're lucky they haven't repossessed it on you or some such nonsense already. You have to show them you're serious. If you're that much in debt, your biggest asset is that beast you drive. Here." She passed her phone over to him. "The dealer over on Rexdale by the 401 is doing a buy-back and lease-to-own thing. You should get several grand and still have a set of wheels."

He quirked his split eyebrow and checked out the site. "That might just work…"

"I'll leave you to it, then." She snatched her phone back, put the screen to sleep, and stood up.

"Wait, where are you going?"

"Home. Where do you think?"

He scrambled up, that desperate look back in his eyes. Josh grabbed her hand before she reached the door.

"Don't go."

She turned back. "And why the hell should I stay?"

"I don't have anyone else. I need your help. And… and I'm sorry."

"Sorry for what exactly? Dragging me into this asinine mess?"

"No. Yes, but no. For what happened in grade nine. It was a misunderstanding."

She sliced the air in front of her throat, cutting him off again.

"Please. I can't do this alone."

They stared at each other for a long time, neither saying or moving or doing anything. Josh still held Amber's hand, a lot like he used to before everything went to shit. Before he turned into an asshole and destroyed her life… well, her high school life. There were so many reasons to tell him to go shove it. To teach him a lesson. Kick him to the curb. This was her time for revenge… to finally get even.

Josh took a breath in and held it.

He was a jerk, but she wasn't. At least, she didn't think so; she didn't want to be that person.

"Okay. Put your shoes on. Let's do this thing before I change my mind."

8

LET'S MAKE A DEAL

Josh's gaze shifted from the partially rolled rug to the sideways wingback chair and overturned coffee table bereft of the jade statue. They'd nabbed the Shoji screen his mom ordered on her last trip to Japan, and most of the artwork on the main floor. His guts twisted as he shut the door to the garage. Amber's stare burned into his back. He shifted off his sore ankle and looked up.

"I'll clean when we get back," he said, shuffling the keys to his other hand for extra leverage on the short rail down the stairs to the garage floor.

"Mmhmm." Her noncommittal response punctuated Amber's lack of trust in him. He didn't blame her; he just wished she'd let him explain. She still didn't want to talk about what happened between them in grade nine. He'd tried to sound sincere, but maybe she didn't realize exactly what he'd apologized for.

He sighed and hobbled toward the truck. The sooner they got this mess straightened out, the better. Amber's plan might actually work. Josh reached for the driver's door and Amber hip-checked him out of the way, nabbing his keys at the same time.

"I don't think so, buddy." She lifted her chin indicating Josh get in the passenger side. He scowled. She grabbed the side-mirror and tilted it toward him; it reflected his bruised and battered face. His limp only punctuated her point. He wasn't fit to drive. Josh glared at her, swallowing his pride before hobbling around to the other side of the truck. He climbed in and hit the garage door opener clipped to the visor. Bright afternoon sunlight breached past the rolling door.

Amber waited until the door stopped before easing the shifter into gear and reversing out. She didn't have to adjust much, Josh was only a couple inches taller than her.

The vehicle's warning bell dinged repeatedly. She glanced over at him and stopped the truck at the end of the driveway. He sighed and pulled his seatbelt on. Amber shook her head, clearly in no mood to argue with him about ignored Driver's Ed training and defensive driving. He usually slid the belt on at the end of the street. A bad habit, but it had allowed him to jump from the truck after Saul's guys ran him off the road.

They took Martin Grove over to Rexdale Blvd but the lights stopped her before she reached the dealership. Amber glanced in the rear-view and side mirrors. She nudged Josh. Gingerly, he twisted and look out the back window. A black SUV with tinted windows sat in the turning lane.

"It's probably nothing," he said, that familiar twitch nudging the back of his gut.

She nodded, still refusing to talk to him.

He hoped it was nothing. *Let it go, already. No one's following us. We're just on edge.*

The light turned green and Amber maneuvered over to the Chrysler Dealership on the north side of the road. She pulled in and found a guest parking spot.

"Let me do all the talking," Josh said. If this was going to happen, it would be with him at the helm.

"Wouldn't have it any other way."

As they parked, Josh pulled down the passenger visor and checked his reflection. He straightened his hair, but there was nothing he could do about the bruises. His ire rose. If he could just tap into the special account his parents made him open – but that was money to pay them back for last time. This was a whole new problem.

Amber followed him out of the vehicle. The settling chill of the late-afternoon air nipped at his ears. She walked in with him, but, before a salesman could target him, Amber grabbed his arm.

"Get the most money you can and then work out a deal for–"

"I know." He pulled away, sick of everyone second-guessing him. Jimmy's voice echoed in his head. *She isn't worth it man.* But even when he'd said it five and a half years ago it hadn't rung true.

A pert blonde in a pencil skirt met Josh half-way across the showroom floor. Amber shook her head, sat down in the service waiting area, and watched a little boy play. The kid's dad flipped through a car magazine. A black Caravan pulled up to the service bay doors just on the other side of the wall of windows. The fist in Josh's stomach clenched and twisted. He tried to swallow past a dry throat.

"What can I do for you today?" the saleswoman asked. She tilted her chin just enough to cause her wavy hair to cascade around her shoulders and revealed the smooth line of her neck. He knew she wasn't flirting, he looked like shit, but she knew how to keep a man's attention.

"I'm looking to sell my Silverado, maybe get a lease instead."

"Sure thing. Why don't you show me your truck?"

He nodded and tried not to hobble too much as they walked back outside for the tour.

Twenty minutes later, Josh flopped down beside Amber, startling her from her musings. He held a contract.

"You figured something out?" she asked.

"Yeah. Take a look."

"You haven't signed yet?" Amber leaned forward and glanced at the paperwork in his hands. Her nearness sent a thrill through him. She smelled like honeydew melon. She always had. He shook himself out of the past.

"No. She told me to think about it."

"Really? If it's a good deal, why not just do it? Get the money and run?"

He scrunched up his nose then showed her the contract. "They'll buy back my Silverado for twelve grand."

"Nice."

"But… they won't let me spend it on another buy-back vehicle or put it toward a lease. The deal is only good if I get a new vehicle, and that means my monthly payments go up."

"Okay. But you said your dad gave you a raise. Won't that help?"

"In theory, yes. But I'd have to put ten grand down which means I'd only be walking out of here with two Gs." Josh bit the inside of his cheek. He needed a hell of a lot more than that. She read his mind.

"How much do you need?"

He sighed. "Ten grand."

She pulled away, surprised, but said, "So, just take the buy-back and we'll look for a private sale on Autotrader."

"I'll only get a clunker for two grand." Every muscle in his body went rigid. He had to force himself to unclench his jaw.

"What about going to Cash 4 You around the corner and getting an advance on your next paycheque?"

"I suppose. It'll still be a clunker." A clunker. *Your vehicle sets the precedence for the kind of man you are, the kind of man you'll become,* his father's voice rang in his head. *I'm not a piece of garbage.*

"But you'll be out of debt and you can save up for something better after you pay your parents back."

He blanched. She was right. This wasn't about keeping up appearances. Saul's guys had trashed his home, beaten him to within an inch of his life, and weren't taking "wait" for an answer. *We're done waiting*, had been Saul's message.

"Yeah. Okay, you're right."

As he shifted to stand, Amber grabbed his arm and pulled him back down.

"Josh, look at me."

"What? Why?" His heart blasted into overdrive.

"Just look at me a moment."

"Okay, I'm looking." He locked his green eyes onto her dark orbs. They hadn't stared at each other like that since... well, since before everything fell apart. Before he let appearances matter more than–

"Now, without turning your head, shift your eyes, and look out the window. What do you see?"

She moved her eyes at the same time. The black SUV was still there, exhaust puffing from the tailpipe

"Shit." She'd seen them, too.

"Is that who I think it is?" she asked.

"Yes."

"Why are they here? What do we do? Get the money and give it to them?"

"No."

"What?" Amber tore her gaze away from the window and stared at Josh instead. He brought his eyes back to her as well.

"Finder's fee. They'll take most of it and only hand over maybe a quarter of the cash once they force me to sign the back of the cheque."

Amber balked at the way he'd said "force." Josh was living proof of that kind of coercion.

"Then what do we do? What will they do if you walk out of here without any money?"

He didn't have to say it. She knew. And she wouldn't call the cops like she'd threatened to so many times before because, technically, those men outside hadn't done anything yet. At least, nothing that wasn't their word against Josh's.

The contract wavered in his hands. Josh set the pages down on the seat beside him. "We'll have to run."

She did a double take with her eyes from him to the window and back. "What do you mean *we*? You drive out of here. Go home and lock your truck up in the garage and try again tomorrow. I'll walk home in twenty minutes and never see those guys again."

"I'm sorry," he said, struggling to push past the boulder in his throat.

"I'm not so sure I want this apology. Why are you sorry?"

He took Amber's hands, wrapped her cold fingers in his warm ones, and pulled her to her feet before sliding an arm around her waist. She didn't resist. The feel of her against him ignited so many memories, but he clenched his teeth and buried them. Now wasn't the time. Josh guided her, limping, to the coffee stand away from the sightline of the window.

"They've seen you with me now. I didn't think they'd be back today, but you must have interrupted them at my house, and they felt cheated. One of Saul's guys boasted about it being 'prime picking' time until they heard a car pull in. That was you coming home early. Amber, you have to come with me."

"What are you going to do?" The quiver in her voice shot right through him.

"Raceway isn't the only dealership around. I say we lose them on the street, head over to another dealership, you take an Uber home when we get there, and then I'll go directly to Saul and settle this."

Amber took a minute to think about it. He watched her eyes flicker as she weighed her options, arguing with herself. She really had no reason to trust him, but he needed her to.

She nodded.

Josh gave her waist a quick squeeze then slid away from

her and hurried over to get the contract from the sitting area. Together they walked to the far side of the showroom and Josh explained to the saleswoman he'd have to discuss the offer with his father, since Amber had asked some pertinent questions he couldn't yet answer.

The woman took it in stride and promised to keep the contract and contact him next week if she hadn't heard from him by then. With the nose of the black Caravan in view and, after scanning the area for signs of Saul's lackies, Josh led Amber to the main doors.

"Ready?" he whispered into her ear, his nose touching her soft auburn hair.

"God, Josh… yeah."

They ran. Josh didn't limp but the spike of pain up his leg from the ankle and the one through his chest from his sore rids cost him his footing when she tossed him the keys. He gasped, staggering to scoop the bunch of metal as she deked around the back of the truck. Josh sucked air through the ache. They hopped in and he peeled away.

Out on Rexdale Blvd. as Josh wove past cars and picked back roads with just the right amount of traffic, Amber looked up the location of other nearby dealerships.

"I think we've lost them," he said about fifteen minutes later.

"Okay, head over to Downsview Chrysler at Dufferin, north of Sheppard, and we'll try again."

Ten minutes later, as they neared the large car lot, Josh didn't turn in.

Amber whipped her head around looking from where they were supposed to have gone, back to Josh. "What's going on? Why didn't you turn?" Panic edged her voice.

"Black Caravan just exited the Allen Parkway and is trailing two cars behind us. And a black El Camino is sitting in the visitor's lot of the dealership."

"How?"

"I should have known better than to think I could outsmart a loan shark." He shook his head and dropped his shoulders, defeated. A flurry of finger swipes caught his attention as Amber searched for something on her phone.

"What if we just need more distance to lose them?" she asked.

"How's that?"

"There's a guy in Sundridge who's looking for a 2015 Silverado with decent mileage and is willing to pay up to $8,500. This is a 2016, right?"

"Yeah."

"What if you sold it to him, picked up a local beater for $500.00 and then all you have to do is make up two grand? You've got almost a week, I'm sure you could manage it."

Josh's brain kicked back into gear, along with the truck, as he assessed the traffic and the plan.

"And not by gambling," Amber added.

He glanced at her, confused. If they stopped by Rama on the way back, he'd have the cash he needed within an hour. He frowned.

"That's what you got into this mess, Josh." She was serious. How the hell was he going to get two grand in five days?

He looked at the road and shifted to and fro from lane to lane, back-street to side street until he hopped onto Highway 400 off Finch. No suspicious black vehicles in sight. His mom's voice echoed in his head. *Maybe we shouldn't go.* His father's stern gaze spoke of disappointment and something deeper Josh had never been able to place.

"Okay," he finally said. "Sundridge it is. You better call your folks."

"Why? It's only two and a half hours away. There and back we'll be home before Dad leaves the hospital tonight."

Josh frowned. *The hospital? What?* He struggled to concentrate on the situation at hand even as the look on her face betrayed a hefty dose of helplessness mixed with stubborn tenacity. It electrified his insides. This was his one chance to fix two wrongs.

"If I'm going to make this work, *no gambling* as you so astutely pointed out, I'll need your help to do it. You in?"

Amber stared at him. "In for what?" The caution lacing her voice gave him goosebumps. *Now or never.*

"Five days. Road trip north and back again. Ten grand or bust... and you know who'll be on the receiving end of that." He couldn't help it, he had to leverage everything he could. Alone, he'd mess up. Hell, he didn't even know where to get that kind of money legally.

He hoped her mind flashed an image of his body lying on the walkway to the river; his bloody, bruised, and swollen face as he curled into himself on her basement couch; maybe even the crumpled heap of arms and legs he'd forced himself to endure on the landing of his stairwell to convince Saul's thugs he wasn't going anywhere. She hated him for what happened five and half years ago, but did she despise him enough to see him confined to a wheelchair for the rest of his life?

"All right. I'm in."

9

VROOM VROOM

"Okay, see you then," Amber said, and disconnected the call.

"Did I hear you say he can't meet us until tomorrow? Mid-morning?" Josh asked, eyes focused on the road ahead. After an hour of driving, signs for an ONroute station appeared and Amber's stomach rumbled as icons for various fast food chains taunted her.

"Yeah. He's busy tonight. Not unheard of, being a Friday and all." She sighed and dropped her forehead onto her palm. She'd already called and left a message for her dad on the house phone. She knew his cell would be off while he was in the hospital and he probably wouldn't even think to check for a text message until morning. *God, what have I gotten myself into?*

"He still good for the eighty-five hundred?"

"Seems so. I've got his full name and address now. I'll look him up online and see what kind of person he is. I told him cash or e-transfer, no cheques. They bounce."

"Cash?"

"He said e-transfer is fine. Are you set up for online banking?" Amber asked, all business.

"Yeah."

"All right, then." She waved him off.

"You hungry?" He tapped the steering wheel with his fingertips, drumming out a beat in the abnormally quiet vehicle. They'd turned off the satellite radio while Amber was on the phone.

"Yes, but we're not stopping at a restaurant."

"What? Why not?"

"How much money do you have on you right now?"

"Plenty."

"Cash?"

He squinted at the road, but really it was in response to her question.

"No."

"Debit?"

He sighed. "No."

"Credit?"

"Well, duh."

"Yours or your parents'?"

He got quiet then said, "My folks'."

"Because you've already maxed yours out. How much money can you take out on your parents' card? Enough to make up the rest of the ten grand?"

"No."

"How much?"

"Why?"

"How. Much," she demanded.

"A hundred a week."

"And what does your week run? Monday to Sunday? Saturday to Friday?"

"Saturday to Friday. Why?"

"Then that's a hundred dollars we can put toward your debt."

"But we need to eat."

"How much do you have left for this week? Any idea?"

"I could look it up, but about thirty bucks."

"Then that's what we need to live off for the next five days."

"What? That's impossible. You're crazy."

"I know you think that, but I'm not. Turn off the highway in Barrie. Mapleview Road. It's time you learned how to shop on a budget."

"You make it sound like your family's poor. We live in the same neighbourhood."

"True. But I'm putting myself through college. Dad's money…" She hesitated. "Dad takes care of everything else. So, trust me. I know how to stretch a twenty. With thirty, we'll eat like kings."

"You're lying. I know you are."

Amber shrugged her shoulders. "Maybe. But we won't go hungry."

"What about a place to stay? I figure that hundred would get us a few nights at various Air BnBs. If we spend all our money on food, where will we stay? It's winter. It's not like we can go camping."

"No, but we'll manage." Amber wiggled her phone at him and then went back to searching online. "Now, we need to find you a cheap car that's good on gas and somewhere near Sundridge."

For the next twenty minutes they sat in relative silence. The radio played a forgotten song, Josh drove, and Amber surfed the net. It certainly wasn't paradise, but at least no one was chasing them anymore.

Josh followed the off ramp to Mapleview Road.

"Okay. We're here. So, now what?"

"See that big Walmart over there."

"Yeah."

"Find a parking spot. We're going in."

Amber tucked her phone into her back pocket as she got out of the truck and swung around to meet Josh out front. She zipped her jacket against the cold and gravitated toward the pools of hazy light in the growing dark. Josh absently followed, looking at something on his own phone.

"I've got $35.68 left. I still don't see how this is going to work. We've gotta eat."

"I know. But just because we've gotta eat, doesn't mean we need variety. We just have to get through the week. Not even. Five days. We reach your goal and then feast at home. You can gorm-out on fast food and eat at expensive restaurants once your parents are back in town."

She hadn't intended to be snarky, but a hard edge crept into her voice. Amber wasn't sure if it was because of what happened between them all those years ago or because of his freedom now. Probably both. Josh's shoulders stiffened, but then he shrugged and the light from the store blinded her until her eyes adjusted. Josh went for a shopping cart.

He unzipped his red jacket and followed Amber around the supermarket side of the store as her shadow. He didn't say anything, but she'd notice him hover a little more to the left or right if something caught his eye. Like raspberries. But you don't buy greenhouse berries in the middle of winter on a thirty-five-dollar budget.

She grabbed a bag of apples and a crate of mandarin oranges in the fresh-food section then veered over to the breads and grabbed two loaves marked down fifty-percent. In the meats section, Amber collected pre-sliced Genoa Salami and then shot down the cereal aisle. She tucked a box of Honeycomb under her arm – it was on sale – and nabbed a giant container of Skippy Peanut Butter.

"One last stop," she said, and jogged over to the drinks aisle. Josh arrived just as she struggled with a case of twenty-four bottles of water – on for a paltry $2.97. He still didn't say anything, but walked over and collected it from the bottom shelf for her. Then, she did an about-face and snagged two bags of store brand chips from the rack behind them. Josh quirked his eyebrow. She shrugged.

"They're only a buck each. You did say we had thirty-five dollars."

The hint of a grin played at the corner of his mouth, but didn't reach his eyes. Maybe he finally got just how serious a situation this was. Amber couldn't be sure. She really didn't know him well enough. Apparently, she never had.

"Come on, let's cash out and see how I did." Amber tugged his arm and led the way.

With $6.22 left in the kitty, they feasted on salami sandwiches for dinner in the cab of the truck under a parking lot lamp eighty kilometers from home.

When Josh pried open the bag of plain chips, Amber raised her bottle of water toward him.

"To setting things right," she toasted.

He stared at the bottle for a long time, but she forced herself to wait. He picked up his water and tapped hers. They both took a swig.

"I found a car that I think will work." Amber flipped through the stats with her knuckle on her phone – the chips were kinda greasy. "It's actually at a local dealership not too far from where we'll be selling the truck. Frank should be okay with dropping us off. He seems nice. Over the phone anyway."

Josh sighed and finally spoke, "What is it?"

"A 2001 Toyota Corolla Wagon. White. Ooo! It has roof racks." Amber tried to make light of the situation. "Here." She passed him the phone.

"How much?"

"The seller wants eight hundred, but based on the rust spots I think we can talk him down to five. And the mileage is high. It was his grandmother's car. I bet he's just looking to get rid of it."

Josh went quiet again and seemed to zone out looking at

the image on the small screen. The uncertain set to his face and the hesitant look in his eyes reminded her of the boy she followed around all lunch period that first day of grade nine, until she could build up enough courage to say hi. Amber hadn't seen him that vulnerable in a long time.

"You okay?" she asked.

He shrugged again.

She rolled up the mostly-full bag of chips, tucked it into the plastic bag in the back seat of the extend-a-cab, and rubbed her fingers on the lower leg of her jeans.

"What's going on? Why you so quiet all of a sudden?"

He closed his eyes and leaned back against the seat. The light from above cast angular shadows across his sore face. After everything they'd gone through in the past forty-eight hours, she had to remind herself he'd been severely beaten and had his house ransacked. Just because he'd been insensitive back in high school – an uncaring and ignorant dolt – didn't mean he'd lost all ability to feel. Clearly, his truck meant something to him, even if she hadn't.

"Are you in pain? How are your ribs doing? I've got some Advil if you–"

"No. I mean, I'm not perfect, but I don't need anything. I'm dealing."

"Really? I've never seen you like this before. What's up?" She tucked a bootless foot under her knee and turned to face him.

He kept his eyes closed. "My parents gave me this truck for graduation. When I got it, I felt invincible, like I could do anything, go anywhere, conquer the world. It never once occurred to me that I wouldn't make it. You know? Everything was set, I just had to go through the motions and I'd be right where I was supposed to be." He squeezed his lips together and shook his head. "Now, I have to sell it. I'm not invincible. I've made a mess of things and the only person I have to help me get this straight is you."

Amber balked and jerked her head back as if slapped.

"And I don't even know why you're helping me." He opened his eyes but looked forward, out into the night. "I know what I did, Amber. I know what you went through after we broke up. I didn't start it, but I didn't stop it either. George and Sanj–"

"Josh, don't. I know–"

"No, you *don't* know."

Amber's heart raced and every muscle in her body tensed. She didn't want excuses or the inside track. She just wanted it to be over.

"I need to say this. Look, they misunderstood. I never should have told them about that night. How we almost... It just went too far. Jimmy got it in his head to start calling you Caber. I didn't want to, but when you shut me out–"

Amber closed her eyes. She fought it, but the scene in the school cafeteria flickered to life behind her lids...

"Hey Caber!" A volley of male voices shouted as she walked through the double doors chatting with Tanya.

She didn't know who they were yelling at and she looked around, confused. Tanya whispered in her ear. Amber's face went pink and she stopped walking, staring at Josh and his crew.

The guys stood on the bench at their table, Josh scrabbling on the table behind them, and swung their hips from side to side. "These woods are off limits." They hand-chopped either side of their dicks and jumped down laughing and jostling each other and Josh.

Everyone stared at her. And laughed. Tanya said something but she hadn't registered what it was. Amber turned and ran.

Josh burst out the doors on the opposite side of the café and stood in her way.

She slapped him across the face.

"Amber, wait!"

But she left. And every day after that someone called her Caber and laughed in her face...

"I fell into it like a bad habit even if I didn't believe it. And

I didn't, you know. But you wouldn't talk to me. Hear me out. You avoided me and then, I avoided you. I was on the popularity fast-track and–"

"And I was a liability," Amber cut in.

"You didn't have to be."

He turned to face her, locking stares. She could read it across his face, the words hadn't come out the way he'd hoped. It sounded petty. Still, he'd never seriously dated anyone after her. She just figured he got what he wanted from them and moved on to the next. All the girls in their grade vied for his attention. He'd certainly gotten what he wanted.

Or did he? Was he telling the truth? Should she believe him?

"Why are you here?" Again, the wrong words spewed from his mouth. "I know I asked you to help me, but you've got your own shit going on. You could have ignored me, called the cops, and just left me with the mess I made."

She blinked a few more times than necessary. Josh hadn't been this real in a long time. She hadn't forgiven him, but maybe being away from it all helped.

"I don't think I could live with myself if you were confined to a wheelchair for the rest of your life and there was something I could have done to prevent it. I'm not a sadist, Josh. I didn't deserve to live through hell during high school just so you could build your reputation. You know no one ever seriously asked me out on a date after that? That every guy I thought I stood a chance with I compared to you and sabotaged a potential relationship. God, Josh. We had an amazing seven weeks. And it destroyed me. But that doesn't mean I have to hold a grudge. I'll never forgive you for what happened. I don't care if it was Jimmy or Gord or Sanj, but I'm trying to move past it. I think." Her insides churned as her organs waged an epic battle. Where they got the knives from, she had no clue; she just knew it hurt.

Amber slipped her phone out of Josh's hand and did a

quick search, diverting attention away from the moment, hiding her face.

"It's getting late. Head to this address and we should get there before lights out."

He input the street and number into his on-board GPS. "What is this place?"

"A hostel."

He narrowed his eyes at her before starting the engine.

"It'll be fine. It's a safe place to sleep before we meet with Frank tomorrow. Now, put your thinking cap on. We need to come up with another two grand by the end of the week. How are we going to make that happen?"

10

OPPORTUNITY KNOCKS

After stopping off at the Free Store the next morning, Amber and Josh found some clothes and two tarnished brass candle holders. It wasn't long before they were back on the highway headed for Frank's place in Sundridge. The brass they'd collect and take to a scrap yard to get weighed on the way home. It was something Amber's friend Sylvie had done last summer to earn extra cash for her food card this year.

Amber frowned. She tried not to think about school, about why she wasn't where she was supposed to be finishing her studies. Her fingers absently played with the gold locket around her neck.

Josh wrinkled his nose. "I told you, we should have stopped by the Coin Wash. I can smell those clothes from here."

"Wait until we get farther north. It's too expensive here. We've got six bucks left for laundry and more bread later in the week." She could tell what he was thinking, the way he shot short side-ways glances at her. "And I'm not going to spend any of *my* money on this road trip or on you. You got into this, not me. I'm just trying to get you out of it. And no borrowing from the money we raise, either. It'll be hard enough to earn what you're gonna need in less than a week."

"I still don't see why we have to 'earn it' at all. Gordo picked up some concert tickets last year and when he couldn't go, sold them online for triple what they're worth. We could totally do that."

"No. We're not scamming people."

He opened his mouth to retaliate but she cut him off.

"And we're *not* breaking the law. So forget about pickpocketing lockers at a gym. It's only going to get you caught. You're not a thief and we're not going to add that to your list of vices."

"If we just turn off in Orillia, we could go to Rama and–"

"*No gambling*. I'm not going to say it again. Promise me you'll forget that place even exists." Amber stared at him even though he kept his eyes on the road. "You're in as deep as you are because you couldn't control your spending. I'll not willingly bring you there. Hmm…"

"Hmm, what? I don't like the sound of that."

"Don't be such a baby. On the community board at the Hostel I saw an ad for an app."

"Do I even want to know?"

"I think it was called Oddity. Anyway, it's supposed to remotely link you to lists of local Job Bank odd jobs. If we can pick up a few gigs, I think–"

He snapped his fingers. "Arnie."

"What?"

"Not what, who. My cousin Arnie drives for Uber. He's down south in Miami for the Indy 500. Taking the week off. I could get his ID number and we could use his account. That would earn more than some odd job in a backward hick town."

Amber flashed her phone, not expecting him to be able to read it but to prove her point. "Is that so? Over at Lake

Rosseau they're lookin' to hire a bunch of people to paint some house. Says here it pays thirty dollars an hour for two days. If they're eight-hour days then we'd be pulling in close to five hundred each. That's half the goal right there for a backward hick odd job."

"But we're not painters. Who would pay general labourers that kind of cash? I don't know. It doesn't seem right."

"Oh, for God's sake, Josh. The Job Bank wouldn't have approved it for the app if it wasn't legit. I'm going to fill in an application for each of us. This is too sweet to pass up."

She went quiet for a moment then realized the Uber idea just might fly. It was probably in the contract not to share IDs and such with other people, but that kind of line-blurring might just save Josh's ass.

"And call Arnie when we stop for gas," she said.

Her thumbs zoomed over the keypad of her phone as she filled in the necessary info for herself, then slower for Josh. She had to keep asking him for information. The whole time, he drove with a cocky self-satisfied grin. It lit up his entire face. She missed that.

When they used to battle for the Mario Cart championship until 3:00 a.m. on Friday and Saturday nights; she'd enjoyed kissing that smirk off his face and then tickling him to tears. After last night's confession, he needed something to be proud of and the Uber-thing was by far better than anything else he'd suggested.

By ten thirty that morning Josh pulled into a gravel drive just off Albert Street North in Sundridge. The house looked like a mini-chalet that could use a bit of TLC. A middle-aged guy with a fuzzy orange beard that matched his hair walked out in a plaid jacket and scuffed boots. Frank reminded Amber of the character Red from the old *Red/Green Show*, minus the balaclava. Amber glanced over at Josh. The stern set to his features made her heart drop into her stomach. She placed her hand on his arm but the gesture felt insignificant in the grand scheme of things.

Frank stood about ten paces away, hands tucked into the pockets of his jeans, waiting. She gave Josh's arm a squeeze then climbed out of the truck.

DURING THE ENTIRE TRANSACTION, Josh remained business-like but brooding. Inside Frank's place, he transferred the funds electronically and everything couldn't have gone smoother. Frank even offered to drive them over to Mac Lang's dealership, where he waited for them to close the deal on the Wagon before unloading all of their stuff from the truck's extend-a-cab.

Both Frank and Troy, the sales rep, helped make the transition far easier than it could have been. Troy even agreed to Josh's counter-offer, and Josh was officially eight-grand richer before noon. After signing all the transfer papers for both vehicles and collecting his new keys, Josh walked over to the Corolla and sat in the passenger seat. Amber slipped into the driver's side, and he handed her the keys.

She didn't tease him, cut him down, or ask him why. She knew why. This was officially the end of his invincibility. Amber didn't believe it, but he wasn't ready to hear that either. Instead, she backed out of the lot, waved at Frank and Tony, and headed to the Payday Loans kiosk at the Kawartha Credit Union. The closest one was just up Highway 124, in South River.

Amber stared straight ahead, listening to Josh breathe against the side window as he watched the countryside ebb by. She tried the radio again, but with the antenna gone the resulting static was worse than the silent tension. The stiff set to his shoulders and flexed neck tendons relayed just how unimpressed Josh was about the situation. *Good.* Amber didn't have to feel sorry for him but she knew not to throw something like that in someone's face. Still, it was a hard lesson she hadn't needed four years to learn. The Barenaked Ladies' song "Grade Nine" spat random lyrics into her head. Amber's knuckles went white before she realized just how hard her hands gripped the wheel.

She snuck a glance at Josh without turning. His reflection looked back at her, made her heart leap as if caught doing something wrong. She let loose a long, soft sigh then pulled into the bank's parking lot. A black sedan drove past. Her heart jolted. *No break lights. Relax already.*

Luckily, the bank was open. Josh slipped out of the car and slammed the door shut. The muscles in his back flexed as he stretched his arms to the side and then forward in a physical stretch that likely matched his mental state.

His mood lightened when he climbed back into the car after getting his pay-day advance – another $480.00 added to the tally. Amber took the cash from him until they got to a town with a TD Bank. He'd save the three-dollar charge by not using the ATM here. She recorded the money he'd collected so far on her phone's memo app. Just over fifteen hundred dollars to go.

"So, where to next? The painting job doesn't start until Monday and Arnie still isn't answering your calls. We could hit up the local yard sales and second-hand stores to look for more brass or–"

"Yeah, sure, but we've got somewhere to be by three o'clock. I've also got another Oddity job lined up for us tomorrow afternoon in Bracebridge at the Seniors' Centre."

"Oh? That might be fun. What is it?"

"You'll see."

Amber frowned and then pulled onto a side-road to follow signs for a yard sale. "And what's this afternoon at three?"

"They're looking for people to help out with a booth at the

Arena in town at Winterfest. We get half of anything we earn."

"Cool. Where'd you find out about it? The app?"

"No. The Mac Lang community board." His eyes sparkled and that mischievous grin was back. Amber didn't know whether to be pleased or not.

11

DOUBLE-DARE YA

Josh raised his eyebrows and grinned.

"Oh, no. No way am I doing that. Are you insane?"

Amber stepped back toward the car, away from him. A dark blue van pulled into the nearly-full parking lot of the community centre. He watched as an extended family tumbled out.

"We split the cash fifty-fifty with them." He snagged Amber's hand and pulled her toward the arena, then nabbed the car keys from her and beeped the locks. "I've already texted them that we'll run it for the afternoon. Come on, it'll be fun."

"Hell, no!" She tried to grab the keys back but couldn't shake his grip. "What were you thinking? We could get Mono or Hep C or the flu! And look at you! Who's gonna kiss someone who looks like he just plowed into a brick wall?"

That was a punch to the gut, or the ego. "It's not as bad as it was three days ago."

"Okay, so no blood but the yellow shiner won't win you any beauty prizes."

"It'll be fine."

She begrudgingly dragged her feet past the large

sandwich-board sign listing the South River Winterfest events, games, and booths, and through the decorated side-door. The biggest indoor attraction, other than the free skate, read in large letters: Kissing Booth.

He watched her glower at him from the corner of his eye. Clearly, she thought he was insane. Still, Josh played out his hunch. He knew there was more to her helping than feeling sorry for him. She needed time away for some reason.

At the reception desk sat two little old ladies with an older gentleman standing behind them. The family from the van checked in. The mom took the kids aside and placed coloured bands on their wrists and the grandparents chatted it up with the attendants. The sign on the table clarified: Play All Day Games - $10.00. The dad picked up a bunch of loose skates by their protected blades and followed his troupe through to the arena. Josh squeezed Amber's hand and stepped forward, towing her along. She squeezed back, bone-crunchingly hard.

"Hi, we're here to check in for duty. Rosie, with the Rotary Club–"

"Oh, you must be Josh and Amber! I'm Rosie." The lady on the left sat up straighter and extended her hand, but not before flicking her gaze over Josh's face.

"I apologize for my appearance. I promise we'll take care of it. Amber has some foundation to soften the blow, so-to-speak, and I'll make good use of the props."

Amber glanced at him, confused and a little miffed. This was not going to be a traditional kissing booth, but she didn't need to know that…yet.

"My grandson is nearly finished setting up. Just sign-in here on the helper sheet and check the payment box." She slid a form over listing vendors, volunteers, and helpers, and got to work on standing up. Josh filled in their information while holding Amber's hand the entire time. He knew she'd bolt if he let go. She kept eyeing his pocket with the keys. However, the cutesy look the other lady gave them reinforced that

Amber was at least playing along, if only to save-face in front of strangers.

"This way." Rosie led them past the viewing area to the full rink and up to the second floor. Both doors at the top stood propped open with bunches of balloons to either side. Raucous laughter and loud chatter wrapped around the trio as if they passed some kind of invisible barrier.

People of all ages packed the expansive space. Amber gravitated closer to Josh. He knew it didn't mean anything intimate. She had a thing about strange crowds. The first movie he took her to was a private screening at one of his dad's smaller theatres, near the end of the run. Her eyes had lit up and he was certain she teared up a bit before giving him a hug for the surprise.

A large hand-made sign dominated one portion of the back wall, set higher than all the others. Decorative writing scrawled: *Kissing Booth* in the same bright red lettering as downstairs only with giant lip-prints set on an angle.

"Jerry, my grandson, works for one of those companies down in Toronto that go to corporate events. Well, they were getting rid of old stock and he offered to take it off their hands. We only had to pay the non-profit rate for use of the camera and printer set up. You two know how to work them you said?" she asked Josh.

"Yep. Amber here's a Broadcasting Journalism major and I'm in Business Studies. She can handle the equipment and I can handle the money." He winked at Rosie. She squinted her eyes and scrunched her nose playfully back. Amber's shoulders eased noticeably. The 'kissing booth' was an open party photobooth… not an old-timey *kissing* booth. He caught her eye and raised his brows. She scowled and stuck her tongue out at him.

Rosie left them by the pay table to get her grandson, who was decorating a third hat rack with caps and boas to the side of one of two rows of tables stacked with other get-ups and accessories. Along the opposite side of the booth's greenscreen stood a myriad of cardboard cut-outs of famous people. Josh watched Amber take it all in, but she caught him staring at her, trying to keep a smirk off his face and doing a lousy job of it. She punched him in the arm.

"Ow. What?" he asked innocently.

"You're a–" But she didn't say it – jackass. It had become her pet-name for him over the course of their time together. Rosie reappeared with Jerry.

"Okay, so I'll leave you with Jerry. He'll go over how the booth works and then leave you to it. It officially opens in fifteen minutes. This is our first time having something like this at the fair. People can pick a cut-out to kiss, kiss a loved one, or pucker up alone for the camera. I'll be down at the registration table if you need me, and Jerry will be back later to help clean up. You two kids have fun."

Amber followed Rosie's gaze to her and Josh's clasped hands. She let go and crossed her arms, nodding.

"You can count on us." Josh flashed his sweetest smile, and she waved goodbye. He turned to Jerry, all business. It only took five minutes to go over everything and learn which costumes and props needed the most TLC when handling before Jerry also disappeared into the crowd.

Josh went over to the tables, grabbed a top hat, oversized bowtie and sunglasses, and a large stuffed snake.

"What are you doing? That's for customers to wear." Amber looked over her shoulder at the long line of nobody by the cash.

"Besides the fact that I have a black eye, have you never been to a party photo booth before? Dress up, Amber. Take Rosie's advice and have some fun." He tossed her a jester hat, replete with bells.

"I'm not putting this on." She set it on the table beside her. Josh walked over and stood in her personal space but she didn't step back, keeping her arms crossed between them. He liked it when she dug in and gave him the evil eye – gave her a hot confidence.

"I know what you're thinking," he said so only she could hear. He bent his head low, almost close enough to kiss her. His skin tingled at the memory but he pushed past it when the over-sized glasses slid down his nose.

"And what's that?"

"You're stuck here because of me. You're stuck here because we were run out of town by bad guys looking to send a message." He held her arms loosely. "But they're not here, and the only way I'll get them off my back is by paying them back. So, pick a getup and pretend you're here to have fun. We'll make more money that way. Trust me. Now, I've gotta give my sales pitch to the masses." He gave her a half-smile and walked over to the open space beside the pay table. Before he spread his arms wide, launching into an old-time carnival oration, he glanced over his shoulder at her.

Amber grabbed the Marilyn Monroe wig, giant rhinestone sunglasses, purple boa, and matching wrap-around tutu. He smiled as she dressed up, then turned to the open space filled with locals and made his pitch.

JOSH SMILED FROM EAR-TO-EAR, though only half could be seen around his Phantom of the Opera mask. Rosie and her lovely, also elderly, associate leaned in to almost kiss each of his cheeks for the shot. They'd chosen Paris with fireworks as their greenscreen backdrop. The ladies wore fuzzy feather boas and 20s era flapper hats.

Josh caught Amber's eye.

Her face said, *aren't you adorable,* and lit up with a smile. "In three, two, one!" she said.

The camera flashed, and they actually kissed him!

Amber laughed at the goofy surprise on his face as the

ladies shuffled off to replace their borrowed garb. He quirked an eye at Amber before she moved to finalize the photo on the small laptop attached to the printer. The veil on Amber's hennin princess cone pulled the tall hat forward over her eyebrows as she leaned in to verify the quality of the image before printing. Josh's heart swelled. All through high school he'd hated that she'd closed herself off – from everyone. Smiles had been rare and those he'd caught were purely by accident, only to be replaced by the perma-glower. For the past three hours her smile had grown wider, and quicker.

She beamed as a gaggle of little girls, already dressed as princesses – several as Anna and Elsa – squealed and pointed at Amber. Straightening her cone hat, Amber swept her cape around the ballgown skirt as she stepped from behind the table. Her earlier Marylin costume had disappeared when she saw just how many people brought their kids to this festival. Josh traded off a different getup every half-hour and had his eye on some pirate's gear for the next shift. The oversized patch would hide his black eye and then some.

Amber glanced at the two sets of parents accompanying the six girls and got the nod.

"Oh, my darlings. Where have you been? The ball is about to begin and you don't have your accessories yet. Come! We must get you ready." She swept around the giggling gaggle and helped them try on tiaras, bracelets, boas, and capes as Josh took care of the sale. He knew from the looks on the adults' faces that Amber had made their afternoon.

As the girls finalized their looks in the standing mirror by the abandoned cut-outs, Amber hurried over to change the greenscreen image on the laptop to the castle with fairies and flying pink dragon. But Josh wrapped an arm around her shoulder and gave her a quick squeeze, turning her back around.

"Don't worry. I got this."

She flashed another smile, at him this time, and danced

back to pose with the girls calling for her. Amber got everyone into position then crouched down behind them so as not to steal the show.

"Everyone ready?" she asked.

"Yes!" they all cried.

"Kissy-face!" she called, and all the girls puckered their lips into the air in profile, looking their sassiest for the camera.

"Perfect!" Josh said, and laughed as they swarmed him to see what it looked like on the printout screen. Amber joined them and chuckled along with their parents and Josh as they pointed out where each other was in the photo. Amber pressed print and went to help the girls put their accessories away.

Josh caught sight of Jerry hovering just behind the parents and glanced at the clock on the wall above the double-doors. *What? Already?* The photo booth had been busy from the moment Josh opened his mouth.

Amber joined the girls as they raced back over to their parents, now holding a copy of the printed picture. The group tumbled away laughing and passing the photo around. Jerry walked over with a huge grin on his face.

"I can't tell you how happy my grandmother is. Everyone who got a picture showed her on the way out. That's why she and Dorothy came up at the end – to get in on the action."

"It was a ton of fun," Amber said, reaching to remove her princess hat.

"Wait. Let's get a shot of the two of you for Gran and the Rotary Club. You guys really brought this idea alive." He motioned Amber and Josh to the other side of the camera. "Okay, give us a kiss!" Jerry said.

To hell with butterflies, moon moths invaded Josh's chest. Amber whipped her head to look at him, something verging on frenzy shining behind her eyes. He just smiled, pointed at his cheek, and winked at her. She smiled back. This was for Rosie, not them.

On the floor mark, she placed her hands behind her back, leaned in, and kissed his slightly scruffy, non-mask covered cheek. He inhaled faint traces of her shampoo – honeydew – and closed his eyes, just a moment. Jerry's voice brought him crashing back to reality.

"I'll bring the cash box down if you guys can start packing up the accessories."

Amber pulled away and turned to remove her hat and cape. As if a flag had dropped, the other vendors in the room raced to pack up and be the first out of the parking lot before the rush. The free skate ended in an hour.

They didn't talk as they tidied and put hats and feather boas into pre-marked boxes. By the end, as they left Jerry to pack the electronics, Amber hugged herself. Josh suspected she felt naked now without the costume. Pretending to be someone else had left her carefree, at least for a little while. Jerry handed them two 4" x 6" copies of their picture and set the 8" x 10" version aside.

"Thanks for all your help. Gran has your money for you."

They waved goodbye and headed for the stairs. Josh glanced at Amber's hands lightly swinging by her sides. He wanted to reach out and claim one, weave her fingers through his like they were when they'd arrived. But they weren't fourteen anymore, and the last thing he wanted was to scare her off... Josh had a ten-thousand-dollar gambling debt hanging over his head. He'd blown his chances with her long ago and now wasn't the time to start over.

"There you are!" Rosie gushed as they walked around the corner to the registration table. She gave Josh a hug and he obliged in return. "You kids were just wonderful. The kissing booth was a hit. Here"–she passed Josh an envelope which Amber tugged out of his grasp–"you deserve every penny.

Don't be strangers, now. The maple syrup festival is in April and we'd love to have you back."

"Thanks so much, Rosie. Glad we could help. We'll come if we can, but that's right around exam time, so no promises," he said, and gave her a wink. She waved the two of them off and Josh and Amber walked out into the cool, dark evening.

Their breath frosted in the air. Amber zipped up her jacket and hunched her shoulders. Josh unlocked the car and they hurried to get in. It was still cold, but the lack of wind made it bearable. Josh blasted the heater as the car warmed up.

"So, how did we do?" he asked, rubbing his hands against the chill.

Amber eyed him.

"What? It's an honest question."

She opened the white envelope and took out a wad of cash. She counted the money, her lips moving without sound. When she got to the end, she frowned and counted again.

"What? How much did we make?"

"We got *half* of what we earned?" she asked.

"Yeah, that was the deal."

"Wow. Rosie wasn't kidding then."

"How much did we make?" Josh tried to snatch the cash from her hands but she pulled it away and put it back in the envelope.

"A hundred and fifty bucks."

He whistled. "For three hours worth of work? Nice. And you say this job at Lake Rosseau will bring in five hundred a day?"

"That's what it says. Less taxes and whatever."

"Nice. There's a Quick Mart just down the street. Since we're on a roll, we should grab a handful of instant snap tickets and–"

"No." The joy faded from Amber's eyes.

The change jarred him.

"We are not gambling." She stuffed the envelope in her

jacket pocket. "Head to the bank. I'll watch you deposit what's here and then we can head south to Huntsville."

Amber took out her phone and searched for a hostel to stay at. She bit her lip.

"What?" Josh asked.

He caught her glance briefly before he put the car in gear and pulled out onto the road.

"Nothing."

12
———

THE PORCELAIN GODS

The dark in the north hung more absolute than the dark in the city. Sure, they had streetlights, but the long stretches of highway with nothing else around ate at the soft glow like the fading light at the end of an old movie reel. Josh liked the old films and found it odd to show them digitally remastered on throw-back Thursdays. His dad had a storage room full of old films but many of them couldn't be shown anymore. Not just because of the technology, but the brittle nature of aged celluloid.

Amber motioned with her hand. "Take this exit."

"Isn't this the road we take to Lake Rosseau?"

"Yeah. But go east. It changes from Muskoka Road 3 to Main Street just up the way. The hostel is around the bend on the south side."

"What's it called?"

"Knights Inn."

"I thought it was a hostel." Now she was just confusing him.

"It's supposed to be. Probably both. That's the vibe I got from their website."

Not five minutes later, Josh pulled the Corolla into the

parking lot. Amber drummed her fingers against the back of her phone.

He reached for the door handle but hesitated. "We going in or what?" Another vehicle pulled in and parked at the back row of apartments. Its lights played across a stern set to her features.

She sighed. "Yeah. Let's go."

The cold wind whipped up off the body of water from the other side of the road. Amber slunk as low as possible into the collar of her jacket, pushing her fists into her pockets. Josh did the same. The hum of the traffic from the highway sounded more like a distant generator than high-speed vehicles. Otherwise the weight of the quiet matched the heft of the darkness. They walked into the basic accommodations and over to the registration desk. The middle-aged perm behind the counter looked up from her phone. Josh waited for her to snap gum and fulfill every '80s stereotype he'd ever seen in the movies.

She didn't. But she did narrow her eyes – right at him and his shiner.

Not good.

"What can I do for you?" the perm asked.

"We heard this was a youth hostel. We were hoping for a room," Amber said.

"Twenty-five dollars a room per night."

Josh made a strangled sound. They weren't supposed to be spending money. Her rules. Amber didn't look at him, just held up her hand at hip height below the sightline of the desk. She leaned forward.

"I was kinda hoping we might be able to discuss an alternate arrangement."

"Is that so? And why's that? I saw you drive in. You got money for a car? For gas? What do you take me for?"

No employee in the history of the world would speak like that to a customer – at least not in a first-world country.

She had to be a manager, or maybe even the owner. If his studies had taught him anything, it was that she didn't want them there. Either that or she'd never gone to school for the job.

"A businesswoman who cares enough to offer discounted rooms to student travellers. Please, hear me out."

The woman leaned back in her chair and crossed her arms.

"Josh, give us a minute, would you?"

"What? Leave?" He didn't like the sound of that.

Amber turned to lock gazes with him and nodded. He shrugged and stepped outside. But he leaned into the door and listened.

"You don't want to hear our story. I'm sure you've heard them all. Instead, here's my offer. We can work for our stay. We can help in the kitchen, we can clean empty rooms, take garbage out to the dumpster – you name it. Work us until midnight if that's what it takes. Make us clean toilets. We're not here to freeload, but we do need help. We'll share a room. One of us can sleep on the floor if it comes to that, just so long as we've got a roof over our heads and a warm place to stay. We'll be out of your hair by seven and leave the room spotless. We're not here to make trouble. In fact, I'm trying to get him out of it. And he's in deep."

As Josh leaned closer to hear better, a pair of large beefy hands grabbed him and pushed him away from the door into the side of a car.

"What the–"

Two menacing figures crowded around him. He couldn't see their faces, but the soft glow of the parking lot lights made a halo around them.

"Where's the money," the heavy-set guy said.

"I'm working on it."

"No, you shit-for-brains, the money for your truck." The other guy stayed silent, arms crossed.

"In the bank. Saul gave me a week. I'll have it all then."

"You said that last time. You've got money now. We want what you've got."

"I told you, it's in the bank." Lightning zipped through Josh, probably the adrenaline mixed with a healthy dose of fear. *How the hell did they find me?*

A fist slammed into Josh's gut and twisted. He collapsed, gasping for air.

The Inn's door opened, spilling light into the parking lot.

The beefy hand grabbed Josh's jaw and squeezed as it forced his head up.

"We're collectin' next time. Flesh or cash, it's up to you." Saul's guy shoved Josh back into the car. He and his partner disappeared.

"Josh?" Amber stepped out and closed the door. The wind blasted her, forcing her back. Josh sucked in a shuddering breath and forced himself to straighten up even as his stomach muscles recoiled.

He shuffled past a couple of cars and hugged his middle, hoping the chill and the dark hid his condition. "She said no, didn't she?"

"I tried. Now we'll try somewhere else." Amber headed for his car across the lot from the entrance.

"What makes you think any of them will take us in? My weather app says tonight is not the night for us to be sleeping in the car. It might be mild during the day, but we're farther north now. We should just break down and spend the money here. You said this was the cheapest–"

"No. We try the other two locations in town and if neither of those work out, we look for a church."

"A church? This isn't Toronto, Amber. People around here are in bed by ten."

"You don't know that. Often the older churches have basements or small rectories that aren't being used anymore or only house supplies. Come on, let's get out of the cold."

She bumped his arm with her elbow. He didn't believe

her. This place was their best bet and this wasn't Toronto. They couldn't kneel on a pew all night pretending to pray to stay out of the cold. Maybe he could look for a shopping centre garage they could park in. At least then they'd be out of the wind.

Another vicious gust pushed Amber into Josh just before they reached the car. He steadied her as best he could, considering, when a voice cut across the lot.

"On second thought, there might be something you two could help me with."

Josh and Amber turned around, glanced from each other to the woman sticking her head out of the doorway and back again. Without a word, they jogged over and burst into the warm entryway.

"Are you handy at all?" the woman asked. Josh recalled Amber's offer to work in exchange for shelter.

"I am," Amber said. Josh elbowed her. "What? It's true. I used to help my dad around the house all the time. It's more than you can say."

"I've helped out behind the scenes at the theatres. What do you need?" he asked.

"I was going to call in a handyman at the end of the week before the weekend rush, but if you two can save me some money, you can share a room and have a hot meal tonight."

"Thank you." Amber unzipped her jacket. "What's the job?"

"Toilet installation. And removal."

Josh and Amber looked at each other and then back at the owner.

"My back isn't so good these days or I'd do it myself. I can show you a handyman app I use. You follow it, get the job done, and we're even. Deal?" She didn't extend her hand, just raised her chin and her eyebrows.

"Deal," Amber said then elbowed Josh again.

"Yeah, I'm in."

"Good. Follow me."

The woman led them down the hall on the main floor and showed them their room. They left their jackets lying on the single bed, passed through the modest common room and dining area into the back. Two small white toilets sat side-by-side in a vestibule leading to a pickup and drop off bay at the rear of the property. The owner grabbed a folding dolly from between two metal cabinets and Josh heaved a sigh. At least they didn't have to carry them by hand.

Together, Josh and Amber set the porcelain thrones on the cart and Josh pushed it to a room on the lower level, back down the hall past the reception area and around the corner. His gut protested the effort, but at least they hadn't pummelled his ribs again. The woman opened the door and led them into the small suite. She passed Amber a tool kit and showed her how to locate the app on her phone.

"Drain it. Remove it. Come get me. Here are some rubber gloves." She pulled them from her hoody pouch and gave them to Amber. "The dumpster's out back the way we came." And she left.

Amber tossed a pair of gloves to Josh, knelt down, and turned off the water supply from the tank to the wall. Only, it didn't turn off – it gave a quarter turn and jammed.

"Of course."

"What are you doing?" Josh asked.

"What does it look like I'm doing? Have you really never done anything like this before?"

He frowned and pulled out his phone, about to download the app, too, when it dawned on him. How Saul's goons had found him.

"Put that down and come here and help me. You're stronger than I am. There's rust on the valve making it stick." She waddled out of the way and waited, crouched, for him to put his rubber gloves on and crouch down.

"Give me a minute." He turned, removed the battery, and

took out the data chip, pocketing everything in his jeans. "This is gross, you know." He knelt down, grabbed the knob and twisted. It turned, but with resistance. His stomach also turned. Josh sucked in air and held it.

"This isn't the half of it. Wait till we take it off the flange – that's gross."

Josh managed to turn the valve off and Amber flushed the toilet, letting it drain. He lifted the seat. "There's still water in there."

Amber looked over his shoulder. "Just a bit. What's in the tool kit? We can't disconnect the base until it's empty.

Josh rummaged through the small bag the owner left them. "Just tools, fittings, and a gun."

"Gun? What?"

He held up a long tube with a trigger and pretended to pull it from an invisible holster, shooting it from his hip.

"Caulking gun. You're such an ass. Have I told you that lately?"

He laughed and set it on the sink counter. "Not in the last hour. You're due."

"I'd say so." She jammed her fists on her hips. "Come on, let's get this done."

Three hours later they shuffled back to their small room, bellies full of hot soup and warm rolls, arms aching more than a little. Inside, between the small table and the single bed now sat a cot with blankets and a pillow. Josh tumbled onto the makeshift bed and Amber dropped onto the real one.

"I could sleep for a week." He groaned and pulled the covers over him. "Hmmm... *pillow*." He popped his head out prairie-dog style as Amber smiled and took out her phone. She laid on her stomach and started typing.

"What are you doing?"

"Texting my dad to let him know I'm still alive and doing my homework. I have a proposal due the week back and it's not going to write itself."

"Homework? Really? Not me. Never have any." He rolled over onto his back and placed his hands under his head. His stomach didn't complain any more than usual. It was strange having Amber talk about something so normal as school after what happened outside. But it happened to him, not her. And she didn't need to know about it. He just had to make sure Saul's guys didn't go back to tracking him the old-fashioned way.

"Really? You never have homework?"

"Nope. Well, essays and stuff, but I'm all caught up."

"Why do I not believe you? You know, not all of us will be taking over the family business. I need to keep my grades up."

He went quiet. God, if his dad knew what a mess he'd made...but it wouldn't come to that. He and Amber had a plan. It was so surreal being her with her again.

She kept typing and it drew him away from the expectations and assumptions his father laid at his feet every morning and every night. In a way, he needed to get away, too. Problem was, his *problem* followed him.

"Why'd you come back?" he asked. He hadn't meant to. Was going to ask about her studies.

The typing stopped but she didn't look up. "What do mean?"

"You got out. Were in London or somewhere, my mom said. Had a scholarship and everything. So, why did you come back?" He tried to keep his tone neutral.

She stiffened. "I had to." She opened her mouth to say more, but didn't. "Let's leave it at that." Amber didn't go back to typing, she just stared at the wall, lost in thought. He was right. Something was up with her and he'd hit too close to home. Josh shifted onto his side and propped his head up on his hand.

"What's it about? The proposal, I mean."

She blinked a few times then shook herself. "A magazine

I'd like to run. I need to pull together a complete outline by next week."

"Cool. Tell me about it."

Amber sighed and rolled onto her back. They both stared up at the ceiling for an eternity.

"Okay. I'm really interested in Indigenous Cultures and I'd like to start a magazine that focuses on the unique aspects of the different tribes and regions. I'd like to reach out to the local First Nations artisans to see if they would be interested."

"Interested in what?"

"In being interviewed, featured, submit articles, showcase their crafts."

"You gotta be careful with that." He frowned, thinking about his economics and politics classes.

"What do you mean?"

"Well, not all Native people will see your magazine as an outlet for their culture."

"What? Why?"

"Think about it. The news has been full of cultural appropriation stories. And no one wants to be treated like a charity case."

"That's not what I'm doing." A hint of anger and frustration edged her voice.

"No, of course not. But you need to think about it from their perspective. Here is a privileged white girl who wants to put them on display. You really should talk to a rep or chief about your idea. It's admirable, but you don't want to alienate yourself before you even get started."

She went quiet again. This wasn't what he wanted. The wedge between them grew, not lessened.

"It's an awesome idea, really. Just tease it out a bit more. Tell me about the kinds of articles you would include. Who would be the target audience?"

"Well, I had initially hoped the GTA."

"Why focus out there?"

She opened up about her vision for the magazine with it starting online, not wanting to target an already saturated market, and celebrating art and culture.

They talked for an hour, looking at different aspect of the proposal, before Amber caught him dozing and turned out the light. But he didn't fall asleep. With the sound of her voice came the feeling of normalcy; without it, he only had his thoughts: the screw-ups, the gambling, the beatings, and Amber pulling into her driveway from nowhere, six weeks ago, walking back into his messed-up life.

13

I LIKE BIG BUCKS...

Amber gawked at the enormity of the guest house as she and Josh waited in the vaulted front foyer with twenty other hired hands. The half-hour drive over from the hostel in Huntsville had been quiet but comfortable. They'd looped an old wire coat hanger around the antenna, so the radio blasted news of a continuing thaw with overnight lows in the lower double digits. Josh's cousin had come through with the codes to his Uber account and after two-days work in the estate guest house, they'd be headed back to Etobicoke. Amber might even have a couple days before school started to finish her proposal and do some reading. That was what one was supposed to do over 'reading week' after all.

"Josh Bianchi. Amber Miller," the foreman called. Amber and Josh stepped forward and were handed a map of the house with one room highlighted. "Your supplies are already there. Make sure you trim the walls and do a double coat. Clock out is seven. If you're not done, you don't get paid. John Lincoln and Dan Semper," the foreman called out.

Amber and Josh had made sure to put on a set of clothes from the free store. Amber sure as heck didn't want to get her good stuff covered in paint. And besides, her good stuff was starting to stink. She missed her PJs… and toothpaste. Breath mints and a finger for a toothbrush just didn't cut it. Maybe she'd splurge and spend ten bucks on toiletries for them from her own money. She glanced at Josh as he led them through the house to their room. It had been ages since she'd just 'talked' with someone. Last night had been nice – minus the toilet water, of course.

"This is us," he said. They walked into a chalet-style hall overlooking the lake. Skylights brightened the space with the early morning sun. The panels sat between giant, dark-stained beams. A set of double-wide French patio doors let out to a raised deck as the land sloped toward the water.

The few remaining pieces of furniture in the room sat covered in drop cloths and were pushed away from the walls. Amber took stock of their supplies.

"Brushes, rollers, edgers, tape, masks, opener, trays, and a ton of paint. Looks like we're set."

"So, I take it you've done this before?" Josh asked, staring around at the nearly two-story walls. "I think I see a ladder over there."

"Umm… yeah. I painted my bedroom. There just happens to be a helluva lot more wall space here."

"A-yup. What's the plan then? Are we going to actually get paid?"

"Yes. You pour the paint into a tray and start painting the middle of the walls. I'll tape the ceiling and then start on the edging around the trim. When you're done your fist coat, you can help me finish and then we'll do it all over again. We've got"–she glanced at her phone–"eleven hours. Ten, factoring in breaks and meals. Hop to it, boy." Amber smacked Josh on the ass and grabbed the painter's tape before picking up the A-frame ladder lying behind a long couch draped in cloth.

He yelped.

"Sheesh, woman," he said, and then did exactly as he was told.

They got into a rhythm, working steadily throughout the day, taking breaks only when necessary and stopping for a quick sandwich before hauling ass back to work. This was a thousand-dollar gig. Two-hundred and fifty each per day if they didn't screw up. Amber had no idea whose property this was, but if they could afford to spend that kinda dough on general labourers, they had to be well-off.

Josh came back in from a pee break and placed a new roller on his handle. The other one had started to pile and they'd had to backtrack to re-do a large section of wall.

"You know what the guys are saying?" he asked.

"Do I care? Why do you insist on listening to gossip?"

"My dad always says that if you're not listening to the lowest common denominator, you're the fool when he buys your business out from under you. Besides, I think they're right."

"About what?" Amber kept painting. Josh walked over to her.

"About whose place this is."

She turned to face him, damp roller held aloft. "Okay, I give. Who owns it?"

"You've got something on your face again." He rubbed his thumb under her left eye. He'd been wiping small globs of paint off her all day, but now he was just stalling for dramatic effect.

"Whose place?" she prompted as he went back to finish his section of the wall and Amber turned back to hers.

He gave her a wicked grin over his shoulder. "Goldie and Kurt's."

"Liar."

"Am not. John and Dan said they overheard Mike–"

"Who?"

"Mike, the foreman. Anyway, they overheard him say something about this being a surprise for Kate when she comes to stay."

"Kate who?"

"Their daughter. Don't you follow TMZ or some kind of fashion magazine?"

"No. I didn't realize Kate was their daughter. Wait. This is their place? Why on earth would they want to live in the Muskokas in Canada of all places? They're movie stars. They should be in California."

"This is their vacation home. One of them, anyway."

"Oh, so, now you're an expert." Amber stopped painting and placed her fists on her hips. Josh lifted his roller from the re-done area and turned to face her.

"No. I'm leaving that title to you."

"Hey! I never said I was an expert." She just wanted to get this done right.

"Sure you did. You're the DIY master. I'm starting to think you watch a lot of TV and only say you did this stuff with your dad."

"Oh, now you're calling me a liar?"

He placed his roller in the mostly empty tray and crossed his arms, pretending to be offended.

Amber shifted and caught her reflection in the large wall of glass overlooking the lake. The sun had set just enough to turn it into a mirror.

"What the…" She side-stepped Josh to get a better look at herself. Paint lines of various lengths and thicknesses covered her face like a football-player-apocalyptic-warrior. And it dawned on her. "You"–she whipped around to confront him–"you did that on purpose!"

She fell into the old playful spark without second-guessing herself, grabbed one of the pole extensions for the rollers, and held it out like a sword. "Take that, thou vile villain." And she fainted left with a high-strike before changing direction cracking him one on the rear.

Josh yelped and jumped forward; his eyes sparkled as he scooped up the other pole.

"A lucky strike." He pointed his weapon at her. "*You seem a decent fellow. I hate to kill you.*"

"*You seem a decent fellow. I hate to die.*" She smiled. He remembered her favourite line from the movie *Princess Bride*. Josh had convinced his dad to set up a reel in the smallest theatre at the Cineplex Odeon Queensway for their one-month anniversary date. He later confessed he was stalking her on Instagram and noticed it was her favourite movie.

Before she could even wonder what he might mean by bringing that up now, he lunged. She countered the strike and they battled as if they'd trained for this moment their entire lives. Maybe they had, or at least the past five years. Still, it was time for him to feel her wrath. Amber lunged, releasing a war cry. She dropped her sword and tackled him, shoulder to gut.

He let out a woosh of air and dropped his pole-sword, landing on the flat of his back.

He gasped and tried to hold his ribs. "Wha...?"

"I think not. Payback's a bitch, buck-o." She laughed maniacally, fingers poised above him. Uncertainty flashed in his eyes but she gave him a wicked grin of her own and attacked. She tickled him without mercy: under his arms, between his ribs, along his waistline. Amber sat on his thighs and tickled him until he laughed so hard he cried.

"No fair. No fair! Oh, my ribs. You're wicked, you know that?" He finally caught both her wrists and pulled her forward. Amber's lower body rocked against his as he stretched her arm above their heads on the floor. Her chest met his, their lips a whisper apart as they fought to catch their breath. Her hair cascaded around them, an auburn wave taking her back in time to a similar moment. She inhaled a steadying breath then pulled away, rolling off her *ex*-boyfriend.

"Okay, break's over. Back to work, slave." She tried to keep it light, but her insides churned and flipped, battling against common sense. They finished the room by 6:30 p.m. and still had time to clean up – the room and themselves. It was a good day's work.

They clocked out for the day, hopped in the car, and parked down the road at a campsite for the night. With no hostels or even churches to beg at, they had a picnic in the back of the car – seats down – listening to Amber's playlist on her phone by hazy moonlight. The main area of the camp was closed off until April, and that meant no power to the light posts in the parking lot. They were in their own little world.

Josh lay on his side after having scarfed down his sandwich and two apples. The chip bag lay open between them, but Amber stopped nibbling nearly half an hour ago. Her eyelids drooped and fell shut as the last strains of Mariah Carey's voice ebbed away.

"I gotta crash," she said and grabbed her phone to set an alarm for the morning.

"Yeah, I don't think I've ever worked that hard in one day in my life." Josh stretched, wincing a little. She had no remorse over the tickle fight. She'd had to scrub her face and neck raw to get the dried paint off.

The box in the footwell jostled as his hands brushed it. The brass they'd collected over the past three days clanked. He pulled their jackets from the front and swopped the food bags for their extra clothes from the opposite foot area under the folded-down seat.

"Don't squash the chips," Amber said, rubbing her arms. She hadn't been cold a moment ago, but being drowsy, and with it only just 10°C outside, it made her reach for her jacket. She bundled into her coat then lay on her side with an arm under her head. A good three feet of space separated her from Josh. He laid a spare sweater over each of their legs then stuffed the jeans back into the footwell before rolling onto his back and looking up at the ceiling. Their breath fogged the windows.

As tired as she was, she couldn't sleep. Her mind kept spinning from wondering how she ended up here, to her magazine project, to Fanshawe, but always skirting over being home again.

"I wonder what we'll be painting tomorrow," she said.

"I have no idea, but I bet John and Dan we'd finish before them."

"What? Why?" Her pulse quickened and she raised her head to look at him.

"For fun. Well, that and dinner."

"You bet them dinner that we'd finish painting before them? Haven't they done this before?"

"And that's why they think they're going to win."

She didn't like his smug tone or the self-satisfied look on his face. "What makes you so sure they won't? We have no idea what's on the schedule for tomorrow."

"Exactly. It raises the stakes, but we'll still finish before them."

"You can't know that."

"The odds are in our favour."

"How do you figure that?"

"They spend more time arguing than they do working."

"Arguing about what?"

"Technique mostly. It's actually kinda funny."

"And if they win? What then? I don't think they'll take too kindly to being served peanut butter sandwiches for dinner."

"Like I said, we'll win."

Amber sighed and flopped back down.

Josh changed the subject. "So, this magazine thing you're doing. You planning on making a go of it after you graduate or are you going to be an anchorwoman or something?"

"I'd like to make the magazine work. I'm going to have to get a job first. It's not easy getting into an established market, but I'm hoping that next year's practicum stint will place me somewhere I can keep on. At least for a little while. If not, I'll have to slog it writing freelance articles and maybe get into copywriting to help pay the bills for a while. You? You gonna work for your dad right away?"

"Yep." An edge crept into Josh's voice. Amber didn't know what to make of it. "He's already got me managing the Queensway on weekends. That'll shift to full-time hours once I'm comfortable with everything. Then he'll move Ray, the main manager, over to the Colossus in Vaughan – you know, the one shaped like a spaceship."

"Yeah. I take it that would be a step up for Ray?"

"In a way. It would get him closer to home and he'd be in charge of more staff. Dad's going to have me 'work my way up' over the next ten years before he retires."

"Sounds like he has your life all planed out for you. Is this what you want?"

"Yeah, mostly. I like the industry. Not sure I'll ever get used to hobnobbing it with the to-dos but Dad says that'll come over time. It's a sweet deal."

"But…"

"But what?"

"You don't exactly sound excited at the prospect."

Josh shrugged and stared up at the roof.

"What's your dad going to do when he retires?"

"Probably help my mom with the charity side of the business. Take more vacations."

"Cool. Is it still the two theatres he owns?"

"Nah, we've got three now. He bought out the Rainbow Cinema at Woodbine Centre. He hasn't decided what to do with it yet, but he's letting it carry on with all the same staff and everything for now. Hey, that Gala they hold every spring is coming up soon. Your mom and dad gonna come? We missed seeing them last year. My mom asked after yours when I mentioned you'd moved back home. Haven't seen her around in a while. Said she tried to call a few times but always got the answering machine."

Amber clenched her jaw and swallowed. She shrugged. "I'm gonna try to get some sleep."

"'Kay," he said after a long sigh.

Amber's mother had been confined to a wheelchair just over a year ago when the disease worsened. Walking with a cane was no longer an option. Between her periodic twitching spasms and frequent numbness in her legs, she'd finally agreed to the chair.

She shivered, hugging her one arm tighter around her stomach.

"Hey," Josh said.

Amber opened her eyes.

"Don't take this the wrong way, but we could warm up a bunch more if we got closer… shared body heat."

Her eyes widened.

"Fully clothed. No funny business – I promise. If we make a sleeping bag out of our coats and huddle inside together, we'll be warmer."

She knew that from her Girl Guide days, but did she really want to get that close to someone with a history of ruining her life? Amber trembled again and her teeth chattered.

"All right. Let's try it. I won't sleep if I'm shivering and we've got another long day tomorrow." *I won't sleep if he tries something. Stop it. He's been nothing but a gentleman this whole crazy trip. Why would he risk everything now? What does that even mean? God, Amber, think straight, would you?*

Josh sat up and waved for Amber to as well. He slipped out of his jacket and motioned for her to do the same as he yanked the upper portion of the head rests from the flattened seats and placed them side by side. He zipped the coats together one way and then shifted to the centre of the back, inclining his head for her to join him. Amber slid closer until the three feet of space once separating them turned into a negative one as she lifted her leg over his thigh. Josh pulled the two sweaters over their lower limbs and then curled the double jacket around them, zipping it up the front. They wiggled and scooted down far enough they were able to lay on their sides, heads on the rests. As they faced each other their jackets pulled, cracking some stitching.

"You know, this would work better if you turned around. Had your back to me."

"You want to spoon."

"If you want to be blunt, yes. I think we might save our coats the strain and with our bodies closer, we'd benefit more from the heat."

She sighed. "Fine."

As she twisted and shifted within their makeshift sleeping bag, he created a cage with his arms and she circled around. She rested her back against his chest. His one arm slipped under her neck and the other around her waist. Her body resisted melting into his warmth. She hadn't been this close to a guy since... well, since the night before they broke up. His breath defrosted her ear and played with the tendrils of hair locked behind it.

"You can relax, you know."

"I know," she said more abruptly than she intended.

It was his turn to sigh. "I never wanted to hurt you, Amber. I was a dumb kid who let a stupid thing get blown out of proportion. I should have kept our relationship to myself. The guys... I think they were jealous. I didn't get that back then, but I can see it now. I let things escalate too fast and then I didn't know how to make it right. By then, you hated me, and I'd convinced myself I didn't care. That they were right after all. I meant it when I said I was sorry. If I could go back and change what happened, I would. But I can't. I have no intention of taking advantage of you. You're helping me out of a tight spot and I can't thank you enough for not giving up on me, even after what happened between us."

Slowly, the stiffness oozed out of Amber's back and limbs

and she let her body mould into Josh's. She closed her eyes and breathed in his spicy scent. But him being nice like this didn't help. The walls she'd built up inside to shut out the reality of her life melted along with the cold in her bones. A tear trickled from her eye, skirting around her cheek. It didn't follow the usual tract down her jaw to her neckline. No, this time it decided to take a leap of faith and dropped down onto Josh's arm, just below where his sweater had bunched up.

He shifted, tightening his hold on her every so slightly.

"You okay?"

She sniffled and sucked in a shaky breath. "My parents didn't go to last year's Gala because my mom hadn't learned how to manoeuvre her wheelchair yet. And they won't be there this year because she's in the hospital." Amber's heart and brain warred with her. She risked so much telling him any of this… saying it out loud made it all too real.

"What happened?"

Amber inhaled deeply and held it, but the warmth of Josh's breath on her hair, by her ear, around her body, made it so hard to think straight – to stay cold.

"She has MS. Secondary progressive Multiple Sclerosis. The doctors are doing everything they can but…" She sighed and pressed her eyes into his bicep. He gave her a squeeze and rubbed her arm.

"That's why you came home. Your mother–"

"–is dying. I mean, it's been progressing toward this point for some time and they've stabilized her, for now. But it's highly unlikely she'll be around to decline next year's Gala invitation. And that's being generous."

"You've been helping out your dad?"

"Yeah. Dad called after exams and told me he'd had to admit her. When I phoned her to find out exactly what was going on, she kept complaining about him not eating right and spending too much time at the hospital. I got the hint."

"You just came home?"

"I had to. I couldn't afford to risk losing them both."

"If he'd taken care of himself better, would you still be in London?"

"You know I was there?"

"Our moms did talk, and not just at the Galas."

"Right. I honestly don't know. She might not make it to the end of the semester or she could live to see me graduate – not in person, but at least hear about it. They can't tell how fast it's going to progress. The meds are helping, but only to mask the signs. Dad wouldn't have called me unless things were touch and go. But he doesn't want to scare me, ya know?"

"Yeah, I know."

Josh pulled her close and held her tight until Amber's breathing slowed and she finally fell asleep.

14

REVERSED FORECAST

"You can't be serious. Goddam you, Josh. There goes a hundred bucks. Why on earth did you make that bet?"

Josh placed one hand on his hip, raised the stencil image and closed one eye, sizing up the job. "It's manageable." Really, he had no idea if it was, and Amber's reaction made his gut clench. If Miss DIY didn't think–No. They had to. It wasn't just a hundred they'd lose, but the entire day's pay. He set the stencil on the old overhead projector and turned it on. Between the light grey image of a wheat field, and the sun shining in through the skylights, Josh could barely see a line to follow on the buttery wall they painted yesterday.

"I swear to God, I'm going to kill you!" She turned, poised to tackle him.

Josh picked up the extra-thin painter's tape.

"No. No way we have time for that," Amber said, gaze flitting from one wall to the next as if possessed.

"You're going to free-hand it?" he asked.

"No. Get out your pencil."

"What, me?"

"I'm not doing this all by myself. Just don't press hard. Trace around the darker image on the wall but keep it light –

as light as possible. When we're done this one, you can shift the image over to the other half of the wall and keep going while I outline with the small edging brush. No breaks. No lunch."

"No problem."

Amber scowled at him. "You're such an ass."

"And… we're back," he drawled like a TV announcer.

She scrunched her nose up and tilted her head. "What?"

"You managed to go twenty-four hours without calling me an ass. I think that says something."

"Yeah, you're regressing."

Josh laughed, slid the battery back into his phone and set his playlist on speaker before joined Amber at the wall to trace the stencil. He squinted in the bright light, searching for the slightly darker shade of yellow to follow. The second he'd mentioned the bet with the guys, Amber had freaked out. Josh watched her fume, the scowl she wore all through high school was now back with a vengeance. It's true, if they lost they'd have to buy dinner for two grown men, and the only restaurant in town looked like it came from the pages of a foodie program or one of Amber's magazines. Still, she hadn't seen those guys argue—it was *American Choppers* in real life. So what if he and Amber had less experience, they could win. It was a shoo-in.

Amber sighed as Amy Winehouse sang about doing what she wanted when she felt like it. He gave her a grin, and sang along.

Josh and Amber watched John, the tall older man, dig into his twenty-five-dollar mushroom ravioli (Amber had pointed this out to him when she opened the menu) as Dan ate a thirty-dollar lamb shank. Sandwiches and fruit were great for getting by, but this place made his taste buds sizzle. Everything looked good.

Amber eyed the waiter as he set down her thirty-dollar herb and panko encrusted salmon while Josh bit into thirty-five-dollar 12-hour marinated beef short ribs. Everywhere Amber looked, Josh watched her silently mouth the price-tag that went along with the food.

"So, how did you do it?" Dan, a shorter, stockier guy, asked between bites.

Amber opened her mouth to answer but Josh beat her to it. "It was Amber's idea to go freehand. Not use the outlining tape and just pencil the stencil on the wall."

"Yeah"–John took a sip of red wine–"we did that, too."

"Josh helped," Amber said as she pulled a section of salmon apart. "He–"

"I know how to follow instructions," he laughed. The guys chuckled, too. "Thanks for being such good sports." Well, at least the guys were. Amber hadn't smiled all day.

John waved his fork in the air and gave his head a shake. "Deal's a deal. Even if you only beat us by ten minutes."

"You think that was close." Josh leaned over his meal toward the two men seated opposite. "I was playin' the ponies on the second day of the Queen's Plate and as my pick for the win dropped back a head, rounding the last corner before the final stretch, I could see something cross its eyes through my binoculars. I'd picked the wrong horse. I should have set it as a reversed forecast and made it so I'd win regardless of whether he came in first or second, but I went with my gut and put everything on him to win. And then, as the jockey pulled him out of the turn everything changed within a breath and he pulled ahead to win by a nose!"

Josh slapped the dark wood of the table. The cutlery rattled. A thrill from the memory sang in his veins. "Now that's close. I almost shit myself."

He laughed and the guys joined him. Amber managed a smile but her heart wasn't in it. The manic spark quaking through Josh dimmed during the rest of the dinner, but only just. They traded one-ups for another hour before calling it a night.

Amber zipped up her jacket as the door to the Crossroads restaurant swung shut, blocking out the ambient chatter of the diners. John clapped Josh on the back, towering over the three of them.

"I still don't know how you two did it. This was really your first time?" John asked.

"Amber, you did some work on the backdrop for one of our high school musicals, right?"

She nodded.

"And she's helped her dad around the house. Like I said, I just did as I was told. But, yeah, basically. At least on this scale. So, did you find out for sure if it was Goldie and Kurt's place?" Josh asked.

"Bunch of locals confirmed it. Makes sense with the kind of money they're throwing around."

Amber waited by the Corolla as Josh talked with the guys a few feet away.

"Guess we better call it a night. You two take care," John said.

"You as well. And good luck on the fix and flip. Sounds like it'll net you a tidy profit," Josh said.

Dan raised a hand and John nodded. Amber waved at the two strangers who'd taken them out to dinner. She'd warned Josh not to go overboard on the meal; figured they were likely in just as much a bind as he was and couldn't afford two hundred dollars on a meal. As it was, they'd spent half that on the four of them.

Josh walked over and unlocked the car, a wide smile had him grinning like a Cheshire. He'd banked them a decent meal and now stood a grand closer to paying off Saul for good. Josh glanced around the parking lot – no skulking black vehicles. He sighed and glanced at Amber over the roof of the car. Her frown deepened and she pressed her lips together. They got in and buckled up. The local Moose FM radio station played an old Bryan Adams tune. Amber stared out at the lingering blanket of black. Josh drove in silence back to the parking lot of the summer camp a few clicks east on Aspdin Road/Muskoka Line 3.

They were exhausted and had agreed, prior to dinner, not to drive back to Huntsville until the morning. None of the hostels willingly offered a free night's stay and they didn't want to be fixing someone else's toilets when they were that tired. Amber had suggested St. Michael's Church, just down highway 141, but as Josh had pointed out earlier, this wasn't Toronto. He'd convinced her it wasn't worth trying.

Half an hour later, Amber lay curled against him with his arms wrapped around her, but it felt different this time. She hadn't gone stiff, and yet tension radiated from her echoing her mood over dinner. He wanted to ask her what was wrong but knew better than to stir a hornet's nest. Somehow, having a nice night out amidst all this havoc hadn't cheered her up.

Amber avoided talking and lay awake in his arms far longer than he figured she might. He still couldn't get over the fact she'd agreed to help him. That had to count for something.

15

A LITTLE TOO REAL-LIFE

I f Amber hadn't ignored her alarm the next morning, she might have had a little more time to prepare for her backup plan. Technically speaking, Josh hadn't lost them any money with his bet so they didn't need to make it up. However, a job was a job and they really couldn't afford to pass up fifty bucks each for an hour's work. They could head back to Etobicoke making use of Josh's cousin's Uber service shortly thereafter.

She smoothed down her wind-blown hair as they walked into the Huntsville Art Society building before undoing her jacket. A woman walked out of an office and welcomed them.

"Are you here for the art class?"

"In a manner of speaking." Amber extended her hand. "I'm Amber and this is Josh. We're this session's models."

"I'm associate director Ellen Newberg. I can't thank you enough for responding to our last-minute posting. Our original models were unable to make it and we didn't want to cancel the class. Just a moment." She popped back into her office and came out with a clipboard. "This way please."

Ellen led them down a short hall and opened a small room with another door on the inside.

"Here is the change room. Greg – he's taking lead on this class – will knock when he's ready for you. You'll be asked to pose approximately three times for fifteen to twenty minutes each time. At the end of the hour, you will be invited to dress and I will meet you back in the main foyer with your cheques. I'm assuming the information you provided online is still correct?"

"Yes."

"Here are the printed waivers. Just sign the bottom and hang the board on the hook here." She pointed to the back of the door facing the hall. "See you in about an hour."

Josh and Amber entered the small change room and closed the door. Amber hung up her jacket as Josh read through the waiver.

"Um... Amber?"

"Yeah?" She turned to face him as she removed her sweater to reveal a dark purple tank top.

"You do realize you signed us up for Life Drawing Modeling, right?"

"Yeah, so?"

"So, it says here we need to be naked."

She blanched. Her mouth dropped open. "You can't be serious."

"I totally am. There's a reason we're being paid so well for this gig. Are you ready to do this? Do we need to cancel?"

"That would mean canceling the class... They'd be so pissed." Her heart hammered. *Oh no, what have I done?*

"We haven't signed anything yet. We can still leave."

Amber lowered herself to the bench against the wall by the door to the classroom.

"You don't have to do this. We didn't lose the dinner bet and Arnie's Uber account is up and ready to go."

"You keep saying *I* don't have to do this. Are you going to do it? You're not... I don't know, not embarrassed to show your body to a room full of strangers who'll stare at you for the next hour?"

He shrugged. "I'm in decent shape."

"But... but they'll see everything. Everything, Josh. You want, I don't know how many, people staring at your junk?"

He gave her a sly grin. "That kind of thing doesn't bother most guys. If I do this, I'll have the best story ever. No, I'm good. See? The class won't be cancelled."

"But I already told Ellen we'd – I'd do this. Now I think I'd be more embarrassed facing her than a room full of people staring at my private parts."

"What? How does that work?"

"She's in the art business. I noticed some Indigenous pieces hanging in the front foyer. The Art Society probably has at least one if not more Native artists as part of their group. My entire magazine depends on maintaining good relationships with people like Ellen so that I can help showcase all forms of Indigenous art. If I – if I back out now, I'm shooting myself in the foot for making a potential contact for my business. Oh, shit, Josh. I have to go through with it. I can't afford a black mark on my name before I even get started."

Amber set a determined look on her face, jumped up and took the waiver from Josh, signing it before she could change her mind. Muffled voices on the other side of the door hushed as one masculine tone began the class.

They were out of time.

Josh signed the waiver, hung it on the other side of the door, and popped back into the changeroom. Without a word, they turned their backs to each other and stripped. Amber looked at herself in the full-length mirror with only her panties on. Josh's back was still turned to her, but she took in the smooth muscular lines of his ass. At least it wasn't hairy. *He's gonna see me naked.* Suddenly, having a room full of strangers stare at her for an hour wasn't the problem. Josh seeing her naked leapt to the top of her worries. She'd been chastised, berated, and belittled for not exposing herself to him when they were fourteen. It was hypocritical. It was insane. Her pulse raced.

A knock echoed in the small room.

"I'll go first," Josh said. He didn't turn to look at her, just shifted to face the door. "You ready?"

Amber smoothed her shoulder-length hair one last time and then slipped off her underwear. She'd taken care of herself even if no one else had reason to see her naked.

Josh turned the knob and Amber hurried over behind him, careful not to stand too close. He opened the door and walked in.

Greg motioned Josh into the centre of a raised area to sit on one stool and pointed Amber to the other – their backs mostly to each other facing the circle of twelve easels surrounding them. No one gawked at her, and Greg looked at her as if she were fully clothed. The heater above kicked on and radiated a comfortable, early summer afternoon warmth.

She and Josh were instructed to sit in similar poses – one foot resting on the bottom rung and the other foot on the ground. That meant Amber's tush just balanced on the edge of the wooden stool. Greg got them to rotate their arms and hands behind them and lean against the far side of the stool looking up.

Amber closed her eyes and tilted her head back so it exposed her neck. No one told her not to. At least with her eyes closed she could pretend to be at Wasaga Beach soaking up the rays in a bikini. She didn't have to look at anyone and she could erase the room and its artists from her mind – until twenty minutes later, when Greg's voice broke through her daydream as he asked them to shift to a standing pose.

She squinted into the soft light of the classroom, stood,

and angled her body as directed: looking down, leaning on the stool with one hand, the other hand loose by their sides. He'd specifically said "looking down" this time, so Amber had to keep her eyes open.

The faceless backs of the large canvases made her think of the starkness of a hospital examination room. Only then, she got to wear a gown that at least covered her front. She breathed slow and steady and avoided blowing her dangling hair away from her face. But as she blinked a stray strand from her eyelash, she caught sight of Josh in her peripheral vision. Her breath caught in her throat even as her eyes drank him in.

His olive skin graced him with a tanned hue even in the dead of winter. The line from his ear to jaw to shoulder and down his trim torso to that firm ass and sculpted leg brought Michelangelo's David to mind. The muscles across his back and along his arms voiced a quiet strength, unlike the shouts of bodybuilders. Her breath hitched and her skin tingled the same way it had when they'd first met, but unlike five and a half years ago the boy who'd caught her eye didn't have this body. She shivered in the heat.

He'd apologized. Some part of her knew, even back then, that it hadn't been his fault. The problem was, whether he spread the rumors about her or not; called her Caber first or not; the boy she'd fallen for hadn't stood up and put a stop to it, either. Maybe if she'd just talked to him, it never would have gone as far as it did, but at fourteen the humiliation blinded her.

Greg called for the final pose – the classic perch on the stool with leg crossed and hands clasped on thigh. He didn't specify which way to look or directionality of the head. Amber looked right at Josh absorbing every taut and sinewy line. But *he* turned his head away.

Her chest ached as her mind reeled to process the implication.

Why doesn't he want to look at me?
She gave herself a mental slap.
Why do you want him to look at you?
But she didn't have an answer to either question.

16

UNSPOKEN PROMISSORY

J osh kept one eye on the road and one on Amber as she took a picture of the cheque and made an e-deposit using her phone. He'd begged off using his, claiming it was almost out of power. As he drove to the nearby Boston Pizza to pick up their first Uber fare, the weight of the silence between them couldn't be masked by road noise or music. It hung, palpable, in the air between them.

Neither had looked directly at the other since before getting naked. He couldn't. All those emotions that bubbled over in grade nine resurfaced with just a glance at her creamy skin – skin that had always been hidden under some piece of fabric or other. His guts twisted. The more fares they picked up, the more distracted from his thoughts he became. Still, he managed to watch for a tail even though he hadn't seen any suspicious black vehicles in some time.

Amber had tried to get his attention in the art studio but not since. She even avoided looking at the kissing booth pic held in place by the sun visor. Whenever her gaze wandered up, he caught her jerking her head away to look out the window. He got the impression he'd embarrassed her somehow. She fidgeted with her necklace, sliding it along the chain letting it click as it rubbed. He'd watched her do that so often, even after they'd broken up. Maybe she regretted exposing herself for a paltry fifty bucks.

"This is good," she said, fracturing the tension. "Calculating in two fill-ups, we're up to nine thousand, five hundred, and eighty dollars."

"Great, so we've basically got today to earn five hundred bucks and then we head home," Josh said, glad for the distraction.

"Yeah. I think you're in the clear. Minus whatever you owe your parents."

"My parents?" He frowned, pulling in at the restaurant. Two other vehicles followed him on the turn: one dark blue, the other black. *Stop it. You lost them when you disabled your phone.*

Amber texted their arrival and the colour, make, and model of the car into the Uber app.

"Yeah. Those goons trashed your house and took a crap load of stuff – or had you forgotten?"

His face paled. "Right. I can owe them for the rest of my life. If I don't concentrate on getting Saul his money, that might be shorter than I'd like." Josh swallowed past a growing lump in his throat. *This is absurd. The money's safe in the bank. They can't shake me down for it before I see Saul.*

A redhead in his thirties wearing a thin jacket walked toward the car and gave a little wave. Josh pushed his crazy thoughts away and lowered the window.

"Hey man, you call for an Uber?"

"Yeah."

"Hop in."

They guy slid into the tidied back seat, Amber having put all their stuff in the trunk.

"Hey, what's up? Who's that?" he asked, pointing at Amber.

"Co-pilot. We drive in shifts."

"Right. Okay, can you take me to Happy Tails Pet Resort –
1393 Brunel Road?"

Amber typed the address into her phone's GPS.

"Will do," Josh said. He pulled away from the restaurant
and onto the main road. Amber started the fare and placed
her phone on a holder attached to the air vent above the
radio, in clear view of the backseat. The black SUV followed
them back out of the parking lot.

Business was mostly local throughout the day but after
dinner, during Amber's shift, they picked up three guys
headed for a bar on the outskirts of Gravenhurst. Josh
checked the request portion of the Uber app as the guys
tumbled out of the car.

"Nothin' nearby," he said, then glanced to the road. No
black vehicle. Maybe he was just paranoid. They were so
close to finishing this.

"You want me to drive down Highway 11 until something
pings? Keep heading home? It's not too late. The trading post
just off the highway might still be open. I could stop in and
get some business cards."

"Sure. You might as well get something out of this road
trip, too." He gave her a cautious smile. "But first, I gotta
drain the main vein. Park this thing so I can make a pit stop,
will ya."

"Ugh, like I needed to hear that. Fine. I don't want you
pissing your pants in the car. It might turn off any new fares
we get."

He laughed and opened the door. "I'll be right back."

Josh double checked that the data chip for his phone still
sat in his wallet, in his back pocket. It helped him feel a
smidge safer. A sandwich board sign and window paint
distracted him as he reached for the door: *Talent Contest,
Tonight*. Bright green dollar signs whispered, no hollered, to
him. *Maybe we can finish this now…*

He bypassed the reservation stand where one of the Uber-guys stood flirting with the hostess. It looked like a temporary set-up for the night's festivities. Josh quickly used the facilities. When he came back out a high-pitched, off-key duet sang into the microphone on the small stage. They did a better job than he could, but if there was any talent in this place, they wouldn't be contenders. He gravitated toward the hostess and away from the door, running through every conceivable "talent" he might have.

Only one thing came to mind.

He registered an act, received his number, and sat down at the bar. The hostess nodded at the barman and before Josh knew it, a tumbler slid across and stopped in front of him. Josh looked over at the guy and shrugged his shoulders.

"The talent get one free. You look like a Jack-man," the bartender said.

Josh raised his glass in salute and unzipped his coat. The main door swung open and Amber stormed in cringing at a shriek into the mic as she scanned the bar. Even in the dim interior she stood out like a beacon.

He smiled.

She fumed.

Amber crossed the room and tossed her hands in the air like an Italian Nona might and stuck out her chin. Josh grinned at her and patted the low-back stool next to him at the bar. She didn't sit.

"What the hell, Josh? This isn't peeing."

"No. I did that in the washroom. This is an opportunity."

"I saw the sign out front. You're not going to win."

His eyes lit up. "Wanna bet?"

"No, I don't. I want you to stop spending money, get back into the car, and Uber your ass all the way home. Tomorrow's–"

"I know what tomorrow is. You don't have to keep reminding me. We're almost there. We win this contest and we're a hundred bucks closer to the goal. And I didn't buy this drink. The bartender said it was courtesy for signing up. And I think the next one will come from that fiery red-head over there." He pointed with his pinky finger at a hot forty-something woman with long wavy red hair, cheering on the butcher act happening in the name of karaoke.

"I swear, I can't leave you alone for five minutes."

"Then sit down and join me. The show started only half an hour ago and from what I've seen, we could win this thing. Nobody here has any talent."

"Neither do we, or are you forgetting that?"

The MC pried the microphone away from the singers and said, "Put your hands together for Lisa and Jackie Smith, everyone. The night is still young. We've got another ninety minutes before Darla and Frank crown this month's winner. Next up is Jimmy Fly with his five-minute stand-up."

Amber dumped her coat on the back of the stool and flopped onto the seat beside Josh, arms crossed.

"Hey Miss," the bartender said and tapped Amber's elbow. "A little hello from Pete over yonder." He used the glass to point to a tattooed tank sitting with a harem in the back corner.

"Uh, no thanks," she said.

"Don't worry. He's harmless. Just making his girls jealous. I'll leave it here for you," he said and shifted over to fill another order.

"Go ahead," Josh said raising his glass in salute. "Like the guy said, he looks harmless enough."

Amber scowled at him, grabbed the drink, and raised it with a nod to Pete, instead of Josh, who smiled as one of his lady-friends took notice and jumped into his lap. Amber grinned into her glass. She sniffed the honey-coloured liquid and wrinkled her nose. Josh glanced over at the barman – whisky. Crown Royal, actually. Josh knew a lot of girls who preferred it if they had to drink the hard stuff. Something told him Pete knew that all too well.

One of the guys they had dropped off earlier took the stage and did a stand-up routine reminiscent of Fozzy Bear. He got laughs, but not where intended, and a lot of groans.

The MC held up a numbered card. Josh left Amber sipping her beverage and laughing into the glass. He slipped away to confirm with the MC they were still in the building, and what music they wanted. A wicked grin made his cheeks hurt. Amber narrowed her eyes at him as he plunked back down onto the seat.

"What did you do?" she asked, only half-heartedly. He could tell she blamed herself for not dragging him out of there immediately.

"You'll see. We're up in a bit. Should bring back some memories."

"I'm going to regret this, aren't I?"

He shrugged but his eyes sparkled.

Amber shook her head.

17

DANCING WITH THE DEVIL

O ver the next hour Amber lost herself in yodels, whistling, more bad singing, and even a sleight of hand magic show that got slightly out of hand when a real five-dollar bill got shredded.

"And now, for the final act of the evening, please welcome to the stage Josh and Amber." Nobody applauded until a spotlight lit up a smaller, round stage just off to the left of the MC. A brass pole glistened in the rainbow lighting.

"No." She shook her head. This was worse than the idea of the kissing booth.

Josh grabbed her wrist and hauled Amber to her feet.

"No fucking way, Josh! I'm not doing this."

But he just gave her an impish grin over his shoulder and raised his eyebrows. He pulled her up on stage just as deceptively slow strains opened and Flashdance filtered through the PA system.

Josh slid his hands up his chest over his sweater, pulled the offending article over his head, and whipped it to the floor. Catcalls and whistles accompanied the reveal of his white short-sleeved tee hugging his toned body.

Amber remember this all right.

It was not a talent.

It was two crazy teens, five and a half years ago dancing along to Josh's mother's workout tapes… workout tapes that just happened to involve a brass pole mounted floor-to-ceiling in his basement. They'd dared one another for hours before Josh turned on the flat screen and selected the last workout session – the dance.

He walked behind Amber and wrapped his toned biceps around her, tugging at the hem of her oversized hoodie.

"Are you ready for this?" he whispered in her ear. His breath tickled. His nearness set her skin ablaze as her heartbeat jumped ahead to the chorus, not waiting for the music.

She leaned her head back onto his shoulder, tilting her chin just enough to make it look good for the audience and whispered back, "I'm going to kill you."

Amber felt him smile against her cheek before he whipped off her sweater to reveal a tight tank top. He took advantage of her arms being in the air and ran his hands down the length of them, barely touching her skin. The heat of his palms hovered over the sides of her breasts before splaying his long fingers across her stomach as his palms and his body drew closer and closer to the stage. He took off her shoes and socks in one sweep then stood turning her to face him.

The music picked up tempo and he twirled her away from him toward the pole. In a flash, the workout video played in her mind. At exactly the same time, the image of her standing naked in front of a mirror this morning told her if she could do that, then she could do this. They could be done and home in time for her to snuggle under her covers and never have to think of Josh and their whirlwind relationship again.

She spun around the pole without grace, hands sticking, feet stumbling. But she salvaged the fumble by gripping the brass tight and flipping herself upside down. Josh's fingers curled under the edge of Amber's tank and slid the fabric toward her bra as he inched down into the splits – at least as far as his jeans would let him. He might not be a gymnast anymore, but clearly he hadn't stopped working out. Amber scissor her legs into an approximation of the splits just as he let go of her shirt, leaving it bunched up under her breasts.

Amber ignored the howls and hoots from the audience, swung her body around and managed to straddle Josh's shoulders, her skin-tight stretchy jeans hugging every curve. She ran her hands over his pecs, curving her torso around his head, her breasts pressing against the back and side of his head. Slowly, as the last strains of the down-tempo beat wavered just before the change, Amber grabbed the bottom of his tee and fell back, tumbling away and pulling his shirt free.

What a feeling!

The chorus rocketed through her veins. She jumped up and fell into the long-ago rhythm of the workout video, flying around the pole and using muscles she'd forgot she had.

Every time Josh's fingers danced over her bare skin or he got close enough, the heat of his body radiated into hers, and butterflies threatened to burst from her chest.

And he looked at her.

Stared her right in the eyes as if she were the only person in the room. Stared at her the way she always wished he might – back then and this morning.

As the final strains of the song ribboned through the air, he tugged her away from the pole, twirling her back into his chest. He grabbed her hips, thrusting his against hers in a V-stance and she tossed her upper body into a pinwheel roll finishing with her back arched, head back, and arms wide.

The cheers of the crowd swelled and so did Josh as Amber ground against him when she rolled back up to stand tall. The MC walked over and said something into the mic as Josh waved and then scrambled to collect their clothes from around the stage. She barely registered something else he kept picking up, but with the lights, the noise and the drumroll to signal the judges to the main stage, she lost track of him. Somehow, she made it back to her spot by the bar.

They announced an earlier act, the first one apparently, as the winner of a very tight contest, and handed the cheque over to the guy who won.

Amber breathed hard and wiped a thin layer of sweat from her forehead. She made to grab her drink but Josh caught her arm and pulled her down the hall past the galley kitchen and into a back corner beside an old phonebooth attached to the wall.

He dropped their stuff and leaned into her, panting. Her body arched into his, responding to his touch as he held either side of her face in his hands and stared at her like nothing else in the universe mattered. But he hesitated. Nose to nose she breathed in his scent and did what she had denied her fourteen-year-old self. She wrapped her arms around him, obliterating the last of the distance between them. His mouth found hers. Her body vibrated as her chest threatened to explode.

Her legs encased his waist as she wished they weren't in the dark corner of some hick pub with too many layers of clothes between them. His lips led a trail of kisses to her earlobe. He nibbled at it, sending spikes of pleasure through her before he trailed his tongue down the side of her neck. His teeth grazed over her clavicle. She shivered.

Amber groaned, tightening her legs around him.

Her phone beeped.

It was the Uber beep.

Responsibility warred with passion.

It beeped again.

She wasn't here to fulfill an unrequited promise from her

past. She wasn't here to get mixed up in a relationship with her ex. She was here to help Josh out of a serious jam.

Amber unlatched her legs and stood.

"Just leave it," Josh muttered against her neck, sending sparks through every nerve ending. She forced herself to place a hand on his chest and move him back a step as she reached for her phone in the pocket of her sweater lying on the floor at their feet.

"Come on, we'll get the next one," he said, circling her waist with his arm. "We might not have won the contest but we're not walking away empty-handed either."

"No, Josh. We might not get another fare until we hit Barrie. You have an appointment to keep first thing in the morning with Saul. Let's finish this." Her last words came out more final than she intended. Still, they did the trick. He pulled away and sighed, looking down at the phone in her hands.

"It's someone from the bar." Amber clicked "confirm" and set the arrival time for five minutes. She held her breath in an effort to calm her heartrate, but as Josh straightened himself within the confines of his pants the distance between them made her ache for him even more.

"I'll meet you out front. Gotta make a pit stop," he said.

She knew what he had to do; and she knew what she had to do. She had to walk out into the cool night air, get the car, and get this road trip back on track. Still, part of her rebelled against the idea of having to go home. Yes, it meant sleeping in her own bed again, but it also meant going back to a reality she wanted nothing to do with. At least she could prevent Saul's goons from beating him to within an inch of his life. She couldn't say the same about saving anyone else, though.

The late-night air didn't bring her sensibilities back the same way a sub-zero winter's evening would. It just made Amber long to be wrapped in Josh's arms curled up in their makeshift sleeping bag of jackets in the back of the car.

She unlocked the beast of necessity that had replaced his truck – the physical reminder that he hadn't "made it" after all. Amber could only hope he didn't give up on the dream or himself and fall back into gambling as a way to hide from his mistakes.

After pulling the car around, she got into the passenger seat and texted the fare-request her location. One minute after Josh climbed into the driver's seat a blond guy and his girl walked out and waved at them. They tumbled into the back of the Corolla laughing.

"Hey! It's the strippers!" the guy said.

"Pole dancers, Greg," the girl clarified. "You guys were awesome. It was a close call tonight, but Brock really rocked the house earlier. Did you see him?"

"No, we missed the first three acts," Amber said. "Where to?"

"Casino Rama." Greg snapped his seatbelt on then helped the girl with hers. They both fumbled with the catch a moment.

Amber looked at Josh and shook her head almost imperceptibly. But he saw it. His eyes flashed.

"You guys want to get dropped off out front?" Josh asked, as if telling Amber they wouldn't stick around, just get the job done.

She widened her eyes and shook her head again, refusing to enter the coordinates into her phone. He nabbed the device from her hands. She didn't want to make a scene, so she crossed her arms and leaned into the door. He drove out of the lot heading for the highway. Something told her he didn't need directions to get there, and that scared her even more. It meant that his "habit" wasn't confined to the availability of Casino Woodbine and the close proximity of the racetrack.

Amber checked the GPS and the time – half an hour's drive.

The last dregs of adrenaline from the dance ebbed. But by

the time they made the turn in Washago on the outskirts of Orillia, Amber fought to keep her eyes open.

She had to stay awake.

She had to make sure he stuck to the plan.

She fell asleep.

18

WAGONS AND HABITS AND HORSES

Josh lifted his two cards from the green felt table and set them flat again. The dealer laid out the flop: ace of hearts, five of hearts, jack of diamonds – the Crispin, a five spot, and laughing boy. He had the eunuch and a red fever. Two pair knaves and fives had him sitting better this time around. Everyone called. No one had folded on the flop all night. The turn revealed a deuce. He knew better than to discredit any card. The woman on his left won with a four of a kind last hand – all twos.

Another flicker of movement past the dealer threatened to pull Josh's focus from the game for the third time. Normally, the bright lights, dinging slots, and general hum of a casino never filtered past him in the zone. The guy on his left folded. The older gentleman on his far right raised. It was enough of a mixed bag on the table that Josh met the bet. He was far from out of it yet. He'd bluffed a thousand-dollar hand once at Casino Woodbine. If given the chance, he could make any set of cards sing for him.

The river dropped. J-Bird. His heart leaped. *I've got it.* Three jacks would bring him back with a full house. He remained perfectly still until his turn to bet. He raised everything he had left. Everything except his anchor chip, the one he held onto in order to keep playing. The woman dropped two pair. Josh showed his full house and held his breath. The older gentleman also spread a full house…ace high. Josh's stomach plummeted.

The flicker behind the dealer pulled his gaze away from the massacre on the table to a pair of dark eyes, auburn hair, and crossed arms. Bells ringing, music, and laughter crashed through the invisible barrier and assaulted his senses. He blinked and glanced at the time.

2:00 a.m.

Shit.

He glanced around. No one stood waiting for a spot at the table. He didn't want to leave, two losing hands meant nothing. That round should have been his. Josh claimed his anchor and slipped away, his guts demanding he turn right back around and finish this.

Amber's eyes blazed. An inkling of doubt crept into Josh's chest. He glanced back at the table. She grabbed his arm, forcing him to look at her.

"I can't believe you. You promised."

"I know, but I almost won back all the money I needed to pay my folks off too. Your plan was great, really, but if I'm going to start fresh and get my life back on track, I need to clear this debt."

"You're up? By how much?"

He swallowed and rubbed a hand over his mouth.

"What was that?" she asked, eyes narrowing as she stepped forward, eliminating the last of the buffer between them.

"I said I *was* up."

"So you're down? With what mon–" A flash of insight swept across her features. "You didn't just pick our clothes up from the pole stage at the talent show, did you? I saw flashes of blue and purple. How much money did we make with our routine? Fifty? A hundred? Is that what we're down?" She yanked him toward the door. "Let's get home. A couple more fares in the morning before you see Saul and you'll be back on track."

He shook her off. "I'm not done." Josh rolled the chip in his hoody pocket. He was so close.

"What are you talking about? You just said you lost our tips. Let's go."

Heat rose up Josh's neck to his ears. Amber's gaze followed it and then hardened. "What did you do?"

"I have to–"

"No, you don't," her voice rose.

"Shhh." He waved at her to quiet down.

Amber pulled out her phone.

"What are you doing?" Josh asked, taking a step back toward the table. The round he missed was nearly over.

She strangled a cry in her throat and turned her phone to face him. She'd accessed his account. It read zero. An ache in Josh's chest swelled as she stepped away from him shaking her head.

"I don't believe you. I–I really don't. After everything... I'm going home." She turned and ran, disappearing into the sea of slot machines and gamblers.

She wasn't about to drive off, he had the keys. One more hand and he'd be back on track. He just needed to take it slow this time. Josh turned and walked back to his spot at the Texas Hold'em table and broke his anchor chip. He had this. He was due.

The dealer shuffled a new deck and dealt him in.

AMBER CRASHED through the bank of glass doors out under the long bus awning. The barrage of dings and rings from the nearby slot machines died. Crisp night air bit at her hot cheeks. She stormed all the way to the end of the tall wooden awning and stood at the crosswalk leading back to the parking lot.

"Oooo!" She growled and shook her hands out beside her.

Amber wanted to throttle him. Never mind those goons, *she* wanted to beat him within an inch of his life. The image of his battered face from the night she found him on the river path told her that wasn't true, but he deserved a good swift kick to the groin. She turned in a circle and looked up at the blanket of stars above hoping her tears of frustration would slide back inside her eyes. One deep breath after the other pushed the anger down her limbs and out her fingers and toes until all that remained was an ache in her heart.

She turned back around. Josh asked her to help him because he knew he couldn't do this on his own. Some part of him knew he'd end up here or somewhere similar making the same mistakes all over again.

Nearly ten grand... He'd lost it all. Amber stopped halfway back to the building. She just couldn't internalize it – that much money, gone. A line of gamblers ambled onto the parked charter bus. Two smokers in long black coats puffed away near one of the benches as if they'd never have a smoke again, before tossing their butts and shuffling over to the line. They hunkered into their jackets. It wasn't that cold. They stood a little away from the others, their fedoras nearly touching as they talked.

She shook her head and walked to the line of glass doors. Josh was broke again. He owed a nasty bookie a ton of money and he was about to lose his last dime. Certainty didn't make her feel any better. He wanted it too bad. Maybe she was stereotyping based on Hollywood, but there was a reason the movies showed what they did. Human nature was their trade. Amber reached for the handle just as her phone rang.

"What?" She looked down at it. It never rang, except...

She spun away from the door and pulled her phone from her back pocket and glanced at the number.

"Dad? What's wrong?"

"It's your mom. I don't know–they don't–it might be nothing. No, it's something. They just don't know how severe or if... I had to call. They–I don't understand what's going on. She's supposed to have another four to six months."

"I'm on my way. I'll get there as soon as I can. I'm about"– she checked the time on her phone then put it back to her ear–"ninety minutes away. Love you." Amber hung up and looked around. She could call an Uber. Josh didn't count. No way was he leaving that table without a fight and she didn't have time to argue with him. Besides, maybe he was right. Maybe this was his hand and he'd win back what he needed to pay off Saul. He'd done it before. It wasn't impossible.

She stared at the bus in front of her. Amber's feet moved without her fully realizing what would come next. She climbed up the steps.

The male driver turned to face her. "Ticket?"

"Where's this bus headed?" she asked.

"Do you have a ticket."

"No. Are you going to Etobicoke?"

"Yes, that's one of the stops. But you need a ticket."

"When do you leave?"

"Fifteen minutes."

"Where do I get a ticket?"

He sighed. "Inside."

She looked through the front windshield at the building and just stared at it. "Maybe not." Amber searched online for the charters going to and from Casino Rama. Her heart swelled larger and larger, pushing against her ribs and constricting her lungs.

"You can't just stand here, miss."

"This will only take a minute." She found the right page, filled in her information, and bought a ticket online.

She flashed the digital ticket at the driver.

He scanned it and indicated with his head for her to board.

Amber scrambled through the mostly empty bus to a group of seats about half-way back and fell into the oversized chair by the window. She stared numbly past the two men in black to the reflective glass barrier separating her from making the same mistake twice. This time, though, Josh had only himself to blame. Her stomach tightened along with her chest. For a moment she'd thought that maybe… The fear lacing her dad's voice looped through her mind over and over. She tried to push it away, to think about her project but flashes of painting, tickle fights, kissing booths, and pole dancing only punctuated her father's words.

The bus's hydraulic breaks released and the door slammed shut. It shuddered and trembled as it slowly moved away from the casino and off into the night. She welcomed the change in scenery even if it was blurred lights against a dark night. The distraction didn't last long. She didn't want to think about Josh and what might have happened if he'd stuck to the plan. But that left her with nothing else to think about except making it home before her mother died.

Tears streaked down her cheeks, over her jawline, and along her neck beneath her coat and shirt. She was supposed to have months, not hours. *Maybe even a year if…* But none of that was really true. It was time to stop running. She hadn't wanted to admit it, but when Josh asked her to go on this crazy road trip with him, she didn't just do it for him. She'd been selfish again. Sure, she came home to 'take care of her father' but she continued to use school as an excuse – a way to keep busy. Watching the MS take her mother away from her had been worse than dealing with an entire high school who'd shunned her for being something she wasn't. And now, time had run out.

19

RIDING THE REAPER

Josh dragged his feet across the carpet. The bright lights, dings, and bells only added exclamation marks to his dismal loss. Again, he'd managed a healthy full house. It couldn't beat the straight flush though. *Damnit.* His palm ached around his last chip – enough to open a bet but nothing to support it. He eyed the slots. He could... No. It wouldn't help. Amber was right.

She'd stormed off. He had to find her. Somehow, an apology didn't seem enough. The drive home would either be really quiet or – but he was okay with that. He deserved it.

The chill of the glass and steel vestibule door spiked through his palm into his arm as Josh pushed it open. He didn't see Amber. She probably went back to the car. A charter bus groaned and slowly pulled away from the curb. He glanced up and froze. Amber's face hovered in the window halfway back.

I'm going home, she'd yelled.

He hadn't believed her.

"Amber! Amber, wait!" Josh leaped forward, aiming to hurtle himself in front of the bus. Two sets of large hands grabbed him from behind and pulled him in the opposite direction around the side of the building and into the shadows.

A man wearing a black hat and matching trench coat shoved his face in front of Josh's as the other man held his arms behind Josh's back.

"Wha–" Josh's guts threatened to climb his esophagus and he choked on his words.

"Hand it over, kid," Saul's deviant growled. His breath reeked of cigarettes.

Josh coughed, mouth closed, turned his head, and inhaled cleaner air. "I– what? Hand what over?"

The henchman punched him in the stomach. Josh folded in half, gasping. The guy behind hauled him back up again.

"The money, dickwad. Where's the money?"

Josh couldn't see straight and his thoughts fragmented in a half-dozen different directions: *Why did Amber leave? There is no money. Am I going to die? Three solid hands in a row and still no joy.*

"Hand it over," the lackey said raising his fist.

"I don't have it," Josh forced out.

"What do you mean you don't have it?"

"It's all in my bank account. You don't honestly think I'd be walking around with ten Gs in cash and cheques in my wallet, do you? Man, that's so old-school."

He raised his fist higher. The guy holding Josh's arms held him tighter.

"Tell Saul I'll see him in the morning. I'm not giving you guys anything. You force me to walk into a bank, I'll find a way to set off the ATM alarm." Josh had no idea what he was babbling but the guy didn't hit him again. He did scowl, but Josh could handle that.

The goon holding him shoved Josh away. He landed on his hands and knees. A foot smashed into Josh's stomach. He landed on his side and curled in, arms over face bracing for impact.

None came.

Footsteps shuffled off into the distance.

Slowly, he uncoiled. His muscles screamed at him. His brain screamed at him, too. He'd done exactly what Amber had warned him not to and he'd lost both her and the money.

The chill of the early morning bit into him, compelling him to stand up and get out of there. He checked his back pocket – phone still there. Keys jingled in his hoodie pouch. Josh staggered back under the awning and stutter-stepped all the way back to the car. He dropped into the driver's seat, leaving the door open as he collapsed onto the steering wheel and breathed through the rest of the muscle spasms.

Josh yanked the door shut, turned the car on and headed back for the highway still dazed. He focused on the only thing his mind could handle at the moment – keeping the car between the lines. Everything else just hurt too much.

THE OVERSIZED HOSPITAL elevator lumbered up. Amber pressed the floor button again, three times in a row, even though she knew it wouldn't make the thing work any faster. She shifted her weight from one foot to the other. The sound of her breathing irritated her, and Amber paced the rectangular space to drown out the sound with her steps. What right did she have to breathe when her mother might be struggling for her last breath?

"Hurry up!" she yelled at the ceiling, the hum and shift of the hidden cables ignoring her. *I never should have left. Dad's always downplaying how serious she is. What was I thinking? I wasn't, that's just it. Josh could have blown his money on his own. I wouldn't be confused about hating him–*

The floor ding drew her to the layered metal doors. She pushed and pulled at them until she could squeeze through. Amber bumped into an orderly or nurse, what did it matter?

She didn't apologize, just ran. Down the hall, past the nurse's station, she turned a corner, and spotted her dad sitting with his head in his hands.

A sob escaped.

He looked up, then jumped to his feet.

She stared past him, aiming for the door he guarded.

"Amber." He waved someone away and grabbed her around the waist as her fingers brushed the handle, pulling her back against him.

"No. No I have to get in there." She struggled against him pushing at his arms holding her closer and closer. "No. Let me go. Let me in–"

He crushed her against his chest and tucked her head under his cheek. "Shh, now, honey. It's all right. She's resting. The doctors want"–he held her away from him a moment–"her to sleep. Look at me, Amber. Look at me. Good girl. Listen now, she's stable."

Amber stopped struggling. "Stable?"

"That's right. I–I panicked. I'm sorry. It's just... she's never been this bad before. The episode–"

Amber wasn't sure who moved first, but they landed side-by-side on the two chairs by the door. "Episode? What do mean, Dad? What are you talking about?"

He took a deep steadying breath and tried again. "Your mother has been having small seizures and fits like before, but they've gotten worse. Tonight, she stopped breathing. Just for a moment. I freaked out. The doctor couldn't explain it right away. Shortly after I called you, he gave her a sedative to help her sleep, now that she's past the worst of it."

Amber clung to her dad. She hadn't wanted to hear any of this, hadn't wanted to believe her mother's time had finally come. "H-how long does she have?"

He sighed. "The prognosis is the same. A few months, maybe more. It all depends on your mother and how much pain she's in. She might–" He closed his eyes not wanting to finish the sentence they both knew the ending to. She wasn't dying any faster than before, she was just in more pain and it had stolen her breath away.

Amber's dad stroked her hair like he used to when she was small and kissed the top of her head. She hugged him tighter. At some point during the early hours of the morning she fell asleep in his arms.

20

DEVIL'S IN THE DETAILS

The indicator light flashed, no longer a steady orange. Josh tried to look away but no matter which way he turned his head, he could see the incessant light flicker on the dash. He prayed the car had a good-sized reserve tank but mid-prayer the Corolla sputtered and coughed and jerked under him. Josh switched on his four-ways and coasted to the shoulder of the highway just south of Innisfil Beach Sideroad as his car ran out of gas.

"Fuck." Josh let his head fall onto the upper rim of the steering wheel between his hands. He turned the ignition off, silencing the radio, and picked up his wallet and phone. The CAA card sat buried at the back of the tightest slot in his wallet. He fished it out and dialled the 1-800 number.

His phone beeped at him as he listened to the ring.

"What?" He looked at it. The charge bar flashed red. "No! No, not now."

He held the device to his ear again. It clicked as someone picked it up.

"Hi, my phone's almost dead I–"

A recording spoke over him. "Thank you for calling CAA. All of our representatives are on the line right now helping other clients. Press one if you wish to hold, press two if you wish to leave your number and have the next available agent–"

The phone went dead.

"Double fuck!" He threw his phone onto the passenger seat and slammed his hands against the wheel. Amber had taken her charger with her. Josh was left with nothing but a pile of brass, second-hand clothes, and mostly eaten groceries. His parents weren't due back home until Sunday. He couldn't sit here and wallow in self-pity for four days waiting for them to bail him out again. As it was, his mother would never take another vacation again because of this. His father – well, he'd rather not think about that. Somehow the "disappointment" speech didn't seem so earth-shattering anymore.

Josh sighed, grabbed his wallet, and climbed out of the car. He looked south into the desert of darkness and north toward the illuminated turnoff. He couldn't cross the highway and thumb-it back to civilization. He didn't want to end up like the deer they'd seen up north on the side of the road. So, he zipped up his coat, raised the collar, and started walking.

It took him half an hour to hike back to the turn off and the ONroute truck stop to find a Tim Hortons. The night staff let him use the land line then gave him a cup of coffee as he waited almost an hour for a tow truck to pull up out front and drive him back to his car.

Exhaustion tugged at his muscles. He went through the motions. Gave the guy his card, confirmed he was on his dad's account, and therefore a premier member, and gave him the address to his house.

"What's wrong with the car?"

Josh read the white sewn name tag on his dark blue jacket. Joe.

"I, uh, ran out of gas."

"Well, gee, you don't need a tow. This plan gets you a free

fill-up." Josh knew about the two hundred free kilometers but not the gas thing.

"Really?"

"Yeah, man. Hop in. We'll get you back on the road in no time."

All of twenty minutes later Joe finished pouring gas from a large jerry can into Josh's car. They shook hands and Josh sat behind the wheel once again, exhaustion pulling at him, dragging him into the seat. He angled himself a little better, watched for a break in the minimal traffic and pulled back out onto the road. What did his mother say about small miracles? Right. *Life is a series of a thousand tiny miracles, it's up to you to notice them.* His thoughts flitted to Amber. She had been more than a tiny miracle, but he'd ruined everything she'd helped him achieve these past five days.

Now, he had to walk into Saul's office at 8:00 a.m. with nothing to show for all their hard work. If he didn't, his goons would find a way to break his bones when he least expected it. The caffeine in the coffee he'd downed finally kicked in and Josh's brain went to work on how to deal with his dilemma, running through every impossible scenario. Forty-five minutes later, he drove past the turn for his house and onto Finch Avenue toward his last hope.

The two-story semi-circular building with the glass rotunda made Josh's guts twist. Was 5:00 a.m. to early? *No, they have to be open twenty-four/seven.* He gripped and released the steering wheel several times taking deep breaths before getting out of the vehicle and walking toward the building as the sun broke over the horizon. *Small miracles.* Josh walked under the sign for the Toronto Police Services – 23 Division, and into the glassed-off reception area. The bullet-proof glass made his heart jump. This was nothing like the way it looked in the movies. He shook his hands out by his sides and walked toward the stark counter and dividing pane.

"Can I help you?" The uniformed woman behind the glass spoke through a speaker, her voice tinny and faraway.

"Um, yes. I, uh, was hoping to speak to someone about a situation I find myself in."

"And what's the nature of the situation?"

"Well, I've been threatened with, uh, bodily harm and my house was broken into."

"Did you file a report or call 911?"

"N-no. I was pretty shook up at the time and focused on making sure it didn't happen again."

"You know who broke into your house?"

"Sort of. It's the same guys who beat me up and threatened to do worse next time."

"Who are the guys?"

"I don't know their names, but they work for Saul Blackwood, a boo–a money lender." He'd almost said bookie. Loan shark would also have sounded bad but both were accurate.

"And your name is?"

"Josh Bianchi."

"Do you have any ID?"

"Yes, my driver's licence?"

"That will do. Drop it into the tray in front of you."

He did. She picked it up and walked over to one of the computer stations on the other side of the divider. Josh tried to stand still but nervous energy made him shift his weight from one foot to the other. Maybe this was a mistake? The woman came back and returned his license.

"Just a moment. Have a seat and I'll see who's available to speak with you."

They hadn't kicked him out – another small miracle. Josh just hoped he didn't need a thousand more in order to save his kneecaps. He sat down on one of the chairs against the wall and leaned forward on his forearms. His brain tornadoed information around his head: what he should say, how much he should reveal, if he should lay charges for the break in, if he *could* lay charges or had to wait for his folks to get home.

The thick metal door set in the wall to Josh's left clicked open, startling him. A male officer with buzzed blond hair and broad shoulders filled the frame.

"Josh?"

"Yes?"

"I'm Detective Constable Patrick O'Reilly. Follow me, please."

This time, Josh's heart didn't just jump, it launched into his throat. He struggled to swallow. "Yes, sir." He wiped clammy hands on his jeans and stood up, following the officer through the heavy metal door and into an office. Detective O'Reilly left the door open and motioned for Josh to sit across from him. He did, sitting straighter than he ever had in his life, his chest compressing his heart and lungs all the while. Josh gripped his legs above the knee to keep his hands from shaking. The officer pulled a pen and pad of paper toward him. The stark room didn't appear to belong to anyone – no personal photos, no piles of papers or files save for one lying unopened to one side of the large desk.

"Tell me about your situation with Saul Blackwood," the officer prompted.

"I–well–" Josh swallowed. "He loaned me money for a debt. Four months ago, when I couldn't pay up, my parents stepped in and took care of it for me. I've been paying them back ever since. But, two months ago I needed to borrow money again." Josh didn't want to mention his gambling problem if he didn't have to. It was bad enough he was in this situation; he didn't need the officer second-guessing his motives.

He explained to O'Reilly about the verbal threats when he wasn't able to pay Saul back on time, not being able to ask his folks for more money and getting an extension on the loan – with interest, of course. And he described how Saul's guys followed him around, beat him senseless, and gave him an ultimatum: one week to pay them back or lose the use of his legs.

O'Reilly pointed to the remnants of Josh's black eye and split lip. "Those from the beating?"

"Yeah, and bruised ribs and a sprained ankle."

"Did you go to the hospital? Call the police? Tell anyone what happened?" O'Reilly's tone hadn't changed but Josh suddenly felt like he wasn't explaining what happened anymore, he was being interrogated, passing judgement.

"No. My ex-girlfriend found me. She tried to get me to call someone or go to the hospital but I refused."

"Why?"

Josh held his breath. Did he dare tell the truth? "I thought I could handle it. I–I was ashamed it had gotten that far and it was bad enough my ex had to help me. I wouldn't–didn't want to have to face my parents when they got back."

"And where are they?"

Josh told O'Reilly about their trip and not being able to reach them. Having no other family or friends to help, except Amber. "We did our best to earn the money to pay Saul. His goons followed us north. I think they were tracking my phone somehow. It's the only thing that makes sense. But–but it wasn't enough."

"Are you planning on paying him what you did earn?"

"Um…" Shit. What do I say? "That was the plan."

He raised his eyebrows at Josh.

"I knew I still had to earn back enough money to pay my parents for the last loan and all the stuff they took from our house as interest payment, so I tried my hand at the casino, in Rama, and–" He couldn't say it. Couldn't admit just how much of a failure he was.

"Is there anything left?"

Josh shook his head, eyes cast down. "I have to meet with him at eight. But when I tell him I don't have his money"–he drew in a long breath and held it–"he will follow through with his threat. I–I need to try and strike a deal. My parents will be back on Sunday. I can get his money for him by Monday morning but if I don't make the meeting, try to work something out, his goons are going to follow me around and– and I don't think I'll be walking after they get a hold of me."

"I see. Did you report the break-in?" O'Reilly asked, jotting notes on the page.

"No. Amber suggested I sell my truck, get the money, and pay Saul off before it got this far." He explained how the simple plan that would have solved his problem didn't work out because of the guys following them around town.

"I was supposed to pay him back, get my folks stuff back, and…and hope Amber never told my parents what happened." Josh looked the officer in the eyes, his entire body vibrating from nerves and who knew what else.

"I'm not going to hide away until my parents come home. The second I walk out the door, I'll be done for. I need to face this head-on. I'm going to that meeting in three hours. I'm officially laying charges, if I can, against Saul and his employees, and I want to make sure they pay for what they did. I know it was stupid of me not to call when they beat me up, or when they stole my parents' stuff, but I'm here now. I want to end it and I was hoping the police would be able to help me."

O'Reilly sat making notes for a moment and then dotted the page with the tip of his pen. Josh's stomach twisted and churned. This was his last chance.

"What you're asking for is highly irregular. If we were to conduct a sting to catch Saul and his employees in the act, it would be done by an undercover police officer. We would not put a civilian, you, at risk. You should wait until your parents come home. You should file a complaint against Mr. Blackwood and his employees for assault and breaking and entering. What you shouldn't do, is go to that meeting today."

Josh's heart plummeted into his stomach. His entire body deflated. O'Reilly didn't understand. But Josh knew, even when his parents got home, he wouldn't be rid of Saul and he'd be constantly looking over his shoulder waiting…

He straightened up. Josh was going to do this with or without help from the police. It had to end.

21

NO REGRETS

Amber shifted away from her father's shoulder and wiped the sleep from her eyes. Her locket pressed into her chest. She rubbed the indent and glanced up. A nurse smiled down at them before opening the door to the room beside them. She shut it behind her. Even though it was a soft click, it resonated through Amber's chest all the same. Dim light glowed out of the far window down the hall. She glanced at her phone, 6:37 a.m.

"How are you doing, pumpkin?" She hadn't been called that since high school.

He always called her pumpkin when she was down. It used to bring a smile to her face, but not today. She sighed and just looked at him.

"I know. I know." He wrapped an arm around her shoulders and gave her a comforting squeeze. Fear bubbled up from her stomach into her throat. She swallowed, trying to push it back down.

"What's going to happen?" she asked.

"I don't know," he whispered.

That wasn't what she wanted to hear.

The nurse came back out and stood beside them, the door

still open a bit. "She's awake." Amber and her dad sat up straighter. "Anne is stable and lucid but still tired. She wants to see you." The nurse looked right at Amber.

Amber glanced at her dad. He raised his eyebrows and nodded.

"Me?" she asked the nurse.

"Yes. I told her you were here. She insisted even thought I advised her to rest. Go ahead, but don't keep her long."

The nurse stepped aside but didn't leave. She glanced at dad. He walked across the wide hall and chatted with her, their voices low. Amber stood and stared at the open door and the dim, shadowed room beyond. She'd raced in full-tilt on arrival needing to see her mother, but now her feet refused to cooperate. Maybe because her heart wouldn't stop doing summersaults in her chest. She tried to steady her breathing.

"Amber?" her mother's voice came, almost too soft to hear.

Amber reached a shaky hand forward and gripped the edge of the door sliding first one foot then the other into the room beyond and stood waiting for her eyes to adjust to the low light.

Her mother's dark honey-coloured waves clung limp to the pillow and the sides of her face. Sweat coated her forehead and upper lip. She lay on her back, eyes closed, I.V. bag connected to her hand, heart monitor pinching her finger. Her pale arms rested beside her on top of the covers. Even her face was paler than usual.

"Mom," she whispered.

Her eyes fluttered open as Anne gave a weak smile. Her eyes were glassy but focused. She looked tired but happy.

"Come here, honey." She patted the bed.

Amber closed the door, not pushing it shut all the way just in case... well, she didn't know. They said her mom was stable. Still, just in case. Her entire body vibrated as she shuffled over to the bedside. Amber tried to take a deep breath but only managed a few small gulps. When she drew level, her mom clasped Amber's hand and gave it a squeeze. It was strong.

She squeezed back.

"Dad said you were taking some time off. On a road trip with a friend for spring break. I didn't expect to see you until after."

"He called. Said–"

"He scared you." She sighed and tugged Amber closer. "You came home early."

Tears threatened Amber's eyes, building up around her lashes. "I couldn't–I had to come. He sounded so afraid, Mom."

"Sit." She pulled Amber onto the edge of the bed. "We haven't talked in a while. A long while." They'd spoken on the phone about school and Dad, but that wasn't what her mother meant. They hadn't *talked* since the blow-up. Since Amber said she was tired of not having a life.

"I'm so sorry, Mom. I've been so selfish. I never should have said those things to you." Amber broke into sobs, trying to wipe away the large tears splashing from her eyes. Anne pulled her daughter into a hug.

"Shh, now. Shh. It's all right, honey." She smoothed Amber's hair away from her face with one hand and kept hugging her with the other, careful not to tug on the tubes connected to her. "Look at me. Come on, look up."

Amber turned her head and lifted her chin to look at her mother even as Anne brushed more tears from Amber's cheeks. Her heart-shaped locket tumbled from under her shirt and dangled between them. Her mom rested her forehead against Amber's and danced the golden locket around her fingers. She gave a sad smile.

"While I didn't appreciate your tone, I can't deny that you were right."

"Wh-what?" Amber sniffled. Her mom shifted to one side

of the bed and lay on her side motioning for Amber to lay beside her.

"Everything you said was right. I got to live my childhood and teen years and beyond without having to take care of a sick parent. I got to be a kid. My parents had me when they were older and gave me a lot of freedom growing up. You never got that, not in the same way. If they hadn't passed away, I would have relied on them and not my daughter. Your father–well, he does everything he can. I'm glad you came home to look after him, but I hate that you had to give up your scholarship to do it."

"I never should have left home."

"No, don't say that. You needed to. I just–I'm your mom. Of course, I didn't want you to move, even if it was only two hours away."

"But you're–you're–"

"Dying?"

Amber nodded. "Gran and Gramps lived into their eighties. You had time with them. I wasn't thinking about that. I was just thinking about myself. The here and now. But now, they say you only have six months? I've been gone for a year and a half. There are so many things I–we should have–"

"No." She kissed Amber's forehead. "No regrets, hon. We had no idea the MS would rear up like this. Dad and I and the doctors figured on several years' time. Don't blame yourself. If you'd stayed home, do you really think we would've spent a whole lot more time together? You would've resented being here and we probably would've argued. A lot. This way, I got to talk to you every week and have video chats. I know we didn't talk about much, but you were living. You were getting to do what I did at your age." Her eyes drooped but she still smiled.

Amber took in a shaky breath, no longer crying but still mad at herself.

"Why don't you tell me about your road trip?"

"I should let you sleep. The nurse said–"

"I'll sleep when I'm ready." She closed her eyes and scrunched her nose. "Tell me a story. Tell me about your trip. Let me listen to your voice."

Amber didn't know where to begin. She couldn't tell her what really happened, who she was with. How she felt about him…

But she did. It stuttered out of her at first and then gushed out ever faster.

Her mother laughed and the ache in Amber's chest blossomed into something different.

"I don't think you should have left that boy alone at the casino," her mother whispered.

"I came home because I thought this was it. I didn't want to lose you. I don't want to lose you."

"Oh, honey." Anne pulled her daughter in for one more hug before she said sleepily, "I'm not going anywhere yet. We still have a bit of time." Her voice faded and her breathing became slow and even.

Amber slipped carefully off the bed and stood there staring at her mother. She hadn't been mad. After all this time. If Amber had just opened up and talked to her mom, she wouldn't have had to carry so much guilt around. Wouldn't have felt like she kept running away. Amber slipped out of the room and closed the door. Her dad looked up from the chair, the nurse nowhere in sight.

"She's sleeping again," Amber said, ready to plunk down in the chair beside her father, but he rose so she stayed standing.

"That's good. How did it go?" It sounded like he already knew.

"We talked. I get it now." She swung her necklace back and forth and swallowed the wave of sadness so she could keep speaking. "I was so wrong, about everything. I thought she hated me."

"Pumpkin…"

"You know what I mean. For yelling at her, at you. For leaving and being selfish."

"She had to straighten me out too," he said.

"What?"

"Yeah, I was doing exactly what you accused us of doing. Expecting you to make your mother's condition your life. I chose to make it my life. I love her. I know you do too, but this is different. I promised her when we got married that I would be by her through thick and thin. But she's right. We got to live our lives, a good portion of them anyway, without this burden hanging over our heads. Not like you." He pulled Amber into a hug. "I'm sorry if I scared you. I honestly didn't know what was going on or what was happening and I didn't want this to be–" He choked up.

"I know, Dad." She hugged him back.

He held her at arm's length. "You should go home and sleep. The doctors confirmed that your mom is stable and just needs rest. You can visit again tonight once you're both better rested."

Fatigue suddenly pulled at every muscle in Amber's body like it was waiting for someone to tell her she was tired to actually acknowledge it.

"Yeah, okay. Are you taking the day off work?"

He kissed her on the side of her head then sat down. "Yes. I'll wait until she wakes up again, talk with her, and then come home for lunch and sleep. We can come over together after dinner."

"Sounds good." She yawned.

"Are you going to be okay to drive?" He shifted as if to stand up again, but Amber waved him back down.

"Yeah, it's just around the corner. I can manage to stay awake that much longer." She grabbed her coat from the chair and checked to make sure her phone and wallet were still there. "I'll see you later."

Amber glanced at the clock on the wall above the nurses' station as she passed – almost 7:20 a.m. Her brain fumbled as it tried to remember something. The elevator opened into the lobby, she paid for parking at the terminal by the door and walked out of the hospital in a daze.

It had been a bad episode but her mom was still alive – would still be alive for several months... maybe more. Doctors had been known to be wrong before. Her mom had forgiven her for running away.

Amber flopped behind the wheel of her car and fumbled with the keys a moment before pushing them into place. She turned over the engine but didn't put the Mini into gear.

She'd told her mom about Josh. About their misadventures and his apology. Her mom had agreed that it was a shitty thing for him to do, let his friends ruin their relationship, but she reminded Amber of how young they were. Fourteen and immature and wanting so badly to fit in. Amber had let it consumer her. Had let Josh's friends have power over her. But where were his buds when he needed them most? On vacation. And his parents? On vacation. And Josh?

She glanced at the time on the dash – 7:35. He had an appointment with Saul...at 8:00. Amber fumbled for her phone and called him. It rang through to his voice mail. She didn't leave a message. Tossing the phone on the passenger seat, she put the car in gear and headed home. Maybe she could still go with him. Money or no, he'd need a witness or he might not walk out of there – wherever "there" was.

She pulled onto Mercury Road from Martin Grove, pushing the speedometer well past 40 clicks. As she rounded the bend to Kearney Drive, just past the walkway where she'd found him beaten within an inch of his life, she spotted a Corolla pulling out down the road across from her house. It turned onto Porterfield before she could get a good look at it, but she knew it was Josh. *Why didn't he answer his phone? Oh, shit. He doesn't know about Mom. He thinks I actually left him at the casino after I yelled at him.*

The car made a right on a red, getting ahead of the traffic going south on Martin Grove. She tried to follow but had to wait. Amber beat her fingers against the steering wheel.

"Come on, come on!"

Finally, the light turned and she booked it around the corner and down the road looking for his Corolla. She spotted it ahead passing Rexdale Blvd. *He's not going to the track. Saul's office must be somewhere else.* Amber tried to keep his car in sight, but he turned right onto Belfield Road and disappeared again. She thought she saw him cross Highway 27 but he was nowhere in sight after that. She'd lost him.

Amber pulled into the Skyway Park parking complex and pulled out her phone. She tried to call him again. Again, he didn't answer.

"Gah!" she yelled at the device. "Where are you going?"

Amber pulled up Google Maps and zoomed into the area, looking at all the businesses that popped up.

"Saul could be anywhere." She sighed until a blue flag hovering over a Cash Money shop on Carlingview Drive lit up her screen. She recalled his reluctance to go to one and get an advance on his pay and how relieved he was to be well out of town when he finally did.

"Is that where you are?" Amber had no idea, but she knew she had to try it. Him seeing Saul alone was a bad idea. She hurried over two blocks and pulled into the lot. Josh's car sat several parking spots away from the front door. Amber drove by. The hours stated 8:00 – 8:00 and the neon sign flashed "Closed". She pulled in beside Josh's Corolla and parked. He wasn't in the car. The clock on the dash flicked to 7:55.

Amber turned the car off and went to jump out, thinking she'd race in and–*and what?* She made herself sit there and think a moment. *He's already inside. The sign still reads closed. That's bad, isn't it? But if he had an appointment, whoever's on desk duty might have let him in even before they officially opened. That doesn't necessarily mean he's in trouble. And what if he's not in trouble? Why would he be here if he didn't have the money. Maybe he did what he said he'd do and won it all back after she'd left?*

She decided to wait in the car until 8:00 when they were officially open. Then, she could walk in, sit down, and wait for Josh. If he didn't have the money, they wouldn't be able to break his legs if someone was around to hear.

But 8:00 came and went and no one even approached the door to change the sign.

At 8:10 Amber grabbed her phone, stuffed it into her pocket, and walked over to the building, her chest tight, heart urging her to run in the opposite direction. Josh had been in there for at least fifteen if not twenty minutes. If he'd paid Saul back, he'd be on his way home by now. Something wasn't right.

Amber pulled the handle and the door swung open with a digital bell chime. She stepped into the bright, warm interior. A tall, lanky guy not much older than her walked through the back door. She heard raised voices before the metal slab cut them off.

"We're closed," he said leaning over the high counter.

"But it's after eight."

"We're running behind today. Please come back in an hour." He lifted a section of the counter up and walked toward her. Amber stumbled back into the door and outside. The guy reached forward, grabbed the handle, and pulled it shut again. A distinct click resounded as the lock slid into place.

She frowned. Her skin tingled. Amber hadn't liked the way those voices sounded. She glanced around and rather than return to her car, she walked to the back of the building in search of another way in.

HEAD, SHOULDERS, KNEES OR TOES

J osh pulled the glass door open even though the neon sign blinked "closed". The place didn't officially open for another ten minutes but Saul had a thing about punctuality. A digital chime rang and a skinny, younger guy dressed business-casual walked from the backroom to the long counter dividing the space. The narrow shop fronted a lot of room in the back – offices, the vault.

"We're not open yet," the clerk said.

"I'm here about a payment." Josh slid a black business card from his wallet onto the high counter. Saul's name glinted white with "loan advisor" printed beneath.

"Just a moment." The clerk flipped the business card over revealing Josh's scrawled name. He returned to the back area. Josh reclaimed the card, his chest clenching tighter and tighter. The last time he'd been here in person was when his dad paid off his previous loan. The hard look in his father's eyes was the only shred of emotion Josh could find, and it never fully went away. Now, he was back and worse off than before.

The clerk returned and motioned with his head. "This way."

Josh followed him to a back office, the guy knocked and left him there. A small black surveillance ball glared at him from the ceiling. Under his spring jacket, he tugged at the bottom of the blue button up shirt that didn't quite fit him. *Take a deep breath. You've got this.* He wanted to look over his shoulder for reassurance, but he knew the only thing there was an empty hallway.

The door opened and the short goon from Josh's house filled the entry, eyeing him up and down sucking at something in his teeth beneath closed lips. His dark suit could have been the same one Josh saw him in a few days ago. The guy stepped aside to reveal a large, dark-panelled office.

"Sit," the short goon said and grabbed Josh's right shoulder. His leg gave at the intensity of the squeeze. He stumbled toward the high-backed wooden chair that looked like it belonged in a medieval castle. The man removed Josh's coat and hung it in the corner on an old-fashioned stand. Josh fell into the chair, rubbed his hands over rough ridges in the woodwork of the arms and gulped. He'd seen enough movies to recognize that some kind of restraint frequently visited here. The door shut. Josh glanced over his shoulder as Saul's man took up his stance beside the door, waiting. He turned back to face the expansive desk and noted two more black surveillance balls in the room. Maybe he'd be okay. They wouldn't want any evidence of foul play getting into the wrong hands.

Josh reached for his phone to check the time, but his hand swiped at an empty back pocket. He'd left it in the car, battery still dead.

Dead.

He tried to shake the word from his mind. Saul wasn't going to kill him… but Josh's father might.

The door opened. Josh swivelled around. The other goon from his house and the night of the beating walked into the room followed by a trim man, average height, immaculately shorn and shaved wearing a navy pin-striped suit. Saul ignored Josh until he sat down and leaned back in the decadent leather chair behind the desk, hands folded over his stomach, elbows perched on either armrest. But it wasn't his posture or his attire that made Josh shudder, it was his icy smile and cold blue eyes.

"Joshua Bianchi, how nice of you to drop by. To what do I owe this pleasure?" Saul's voice cut through the room. The taller goon stood behind the boss's chair, slightly off to the left, and stared at the opposite wall.

"You know why I'm here."

"My boys said you took quite the trip this week. They were concerned you might not get home in time to settle up."

"Your boys tried to shake me down three times."

"Well, now, you have to understand. We're talking about a lot of money here, and you have a habit of making it disappear. They were just doing their due diligence to ensure that your debts were paid. No harm done. Now, where's the money?"

Josh fidgeted and shifted on the hard chair. He ran his fingers over the buttons on his shirt. His throat went dry and he coughed.

Saul's eyes narrowed. He leaned forward.

"They also told me the last time they saw you was at Casino Rama."

Josh cleared his throat. "Um, yeah." He unbuttoned his collar and stretched his neck away from the tight fabric. "When your guys broke into my parent's house, they took a bunch of stuff that didn't belong to them. I need to pay my parents back. Wouldn't have stayed otherwise." At least, that's what he'd told himself at the time.

"Where's my money, kid?" Saul tapped his desk with a thick finger. The man's gaze shot daggers across the table. Josh tried to swallow.

"I don't have it," he rasped, sitting up straight. Josh's

fingers twitched. He gripped the ends of the battered chair arms.

"Where is it?"

"Gone."

Saul leaned back in his chair, a darkness shadowing his features. The goon behind him crossed his arms.

Josh pulled at his neckline again, running his hand down the front of his shirt before gripping the chair.

Saul sniffed. "Your extended, extended deadline was today."

"Yes, sir."

"Why are you here if you don't have the money?" Saul made a motion with his finger. The short goon strode forward and hauled Josh from the chair by the back of his neck.

"Wh-what are you doing?" Josh asked. A bubble of panic rose up his throat as he stumbled to stand. The goon reached inside his jacket. Josh's heart pounded his ribs trying to escape. The man removed a short black paddle and switched it on. He waved it over and around Josh in every direction.

"Clean," he said and did the same with Josh's jacket hanging by the door. "All clear."

"What the hell was that?" Josh gasped, trembling. He held his hand to his chest and pushed hard as he took a deep breath. The bottom of the third button dug into his flesh, clicking. The momentary shock of pain focused him.

"Sit down," Saul demanded.

Josh sat.

"Just had to make sure you weren't trying to pull a fast one on us. You wouldn't be the first. So, why are you here?"

"I'd like to be able to walk tomorrow," Josh said.

"Wouldn't we all. But you have a debt you can't pay. We have tried encouraging you to pay up for several weeks now. One might think you need a little more incentive."

The short goon loomed over Josh from behind and the one by Saul moved around the desk to join his buddy.

"I told you already, my folks are out of town until Sunday. When they get home, I can wire you the money. I tried to get it on my own, but that didn't work out as planned."

"How do you know your parents will pay your debt?"

He didn't. Not the way his father had been acting lately. "You'll get paid. They won't be impressed that you stole a bunch of their stuff though. They'll likely press charges for breaking and entering, assault on their only child, and then instead of you getting the rest of your money, which in no way adds up to ten grand now, you'll have to pay them back. My father might not think much of me, but he has a top-notch lawyer ready to jump at will."

"Are you trying to shake me down, boy?" Saul rose from his chair. "You have absolutely no evidence that my associates took anything from your house. When they came to visit you, they did not force the door or break anything while on the premises."

He had Josh there. They'd followed him in after Josh had disengaged the security system, and nothing showed on the surveillance afterward. They'd blocked it out somehow. Probably with another one of those special devices.

"In fact, any items you may have given us to put toward your debts have only managed to pay for the accumulating interest. You owe me ten thousand dollars, Bianchi." Saul made a motion with his chin.

The two goons grabbed Josh by either arm and lifted him up. A portion of the wall on the left opened to reveal a hidden door. Saul stood before a struggling Josh. The goons tightened their grips. Josh cried out and stopped kicking. Saul leaned forward nearly nose to nose with Josh.

"I have no doubt your parents will give me my money," he whispered. "But they have no proof anything untoward happened at your house or anywhere else for that matter. You have caused me nothing but grief from the moment we met. You will now learn to take responsibility for your actions. I have instructed my boys to make an *impression* on you. You thought that beating by the river hurt – brace yourself, it'll be a long time before you're walking again." He stepped back and straightened his suit jacket.

"Wait! What if I work it off? Work for you? At least until my parents get you the money? There must be something I can do?" Fear ignited every nerve in Josh's body. There had to be some way to figure this out.

"I'm a businessman, there's nothing you can do for me. Take out the trash, boys, and make it memorable." Saul turned away. His goons hauled Josh through the invisible door into a stark hallway and out the back way. The double doors to a black van opened automatically. A large metal dog cage gaped at him from inside.

"No! No! Let me go. Let me go!" Josh squirmed and struggled and kicked as they tried to force him into the cage in the van.

Nothing was going right. This wasn't supposed to happen!

"What are you going to do to me?"

"Exactly what we were told – take out the trash. The compactor especially likes bones," the short guy said and punched Josh in the stomach. Josh stopped struggling and curled in on himself.

"Hey! Leave him alone!" a familiar voice shouted.

Amber! What's she doing here?

"It's the girl," the tall guy said.

"Toss him in. The boss wants this done today," the short one grumbled.

Josh's stomach dropped to his knees as they threw him into the back of the van, slamming the cage shut.

"Josh!" Amber shrieked.

He lifted his head as she scrambled to dial her phone. The tall guy marched toward her as she backed away.

A siren blipped and a megaphone blasted. "This is the police. Hands up. We have you surrounded."

Two officers dressed in black tactical gear swooped in and cuffed the goons. Two others stormed into the building looking for Saul and the clerk. Josh didn't know if the voice recorder imbedded on the shirt Detective O'Reilly gave him actually worked or not, but he was glad to see the man's face. Josh gripped the officer's hand and scrambled out of the cage back onto the asphalt of the parking lot.

"Josh!" Amber cried, pushing against yet another officer. The desperation lacing her voice ripped his heart.

"Can I..." he asked O'Reilly and pointed to Amber.

"Yeah. Don't say anything to her. I'll debrief you once we have everyone in custody."

Josh nodded, held his stomach, and jogged over to the officers baring Amber from the scene.

"Amber," he called.

The officers parted.

She crashed into him and they tumbled down onto a parking curb, their arms around each other holding tight. Amber buried her face into Josh's chest. Her entire body trembled. She spoke nonsense with half words and jumbled sentences. He rested his cheek on the top of her head and closed his eyes.

"What are you doing here?" he whispered, breathing in the fresh scent of her shampoo.

"I–I couldn't let you face him alone – without any money, any witnesses. I don't understand. What's going on? What just happened? I didn't even have time to press call after dialing 9-1-1. How did the police get here so fast?"

Josh sighed and hugged her closer. He couldn't believe he'd ignored her and let her leave at the casino. She was what he'd always wanted and he almost lost her again. He didn't even care that she'd assumed he'd lost the money. He had.

One more game wasn't going to fix that. It never did. He knew that now.

"It was time I took matters into my own hands. They beat me, broke into my house, stole my parents' things, and threatened to put me in a wheelchair. I knew if I missed my appointment today, they'd come for me when I least expected it. I'd always be looking over my shoulder and there was no guarantee they'd leave me alone even if my dad paid them off again."

"Again? What? This has happened before?" She stiffened in his arms but didn't let go.

"Yeah, again."

A pair of officers walked Saul and his clerk out of the building. The loan shark stood tall, not a single hair out of place though his hands were cuffed behind his back. Detective O'Reilly separated himself from the group and walked over to Josh.

"Did it work?" Josh asked looking up at the imposing policeman from his place beside Amber on the curb.

"Yes. When you activated the sound, we got a direct feed."

"Did you get what you needed? Is he going to jail?"

"On its own, what you got for us is highly suggestive but inconclusive."

Josh's heart plummeted.

"But when it's presented in conjunction with what happened out here, with the van and his associates, the thwarted kidnapping and all the other evidence we've compiled against him, along with your testimony and others who've come forward, I'm certain he'll be going away for a long time. Now, we just need to get you back to the station for a debriefing and a shirt change."

Josh ran his fingers over the buttons of the blue dress shirt, pausing at the third one. He stood up. Amber came with him, still clinging to him, her eyes wide as her gaze darted around taking in all of the activity.

"Can I come, too?" she asked.

Josh looked down at her and the dark circles under her eyes, the heavy lids, and drained expression. She hadn't looked like that at 2:00 a.m. when she'd found him in the casino.

"Are you sure?" he asked, smoothing her auburn hair back from her face. She held his hand by her ear and looked into his eyes.

"I can sleep later."

"She can meet you at the station. We'll need a statement from her, too, but it'll be about an hour before you can go home," O'Reilly said.

Amber nodded, still looking at Josh. "Okay. I'll meet you there."

She slipped her arms away from him, slowly dragging her fingers across his back and chest. The cool air attacked any lingering warmth with the absence of her body as he followed the detective over to a patrol car. Something had happened to her in the past few hours, something big, and he wanted to be there for her. Hell, she'd somehow figured out where he was and came looking for him even after he'd lost everything.

But he hadn't, really.

The way she looked at him…

… little miracles.

23

VICE RIDE

J osh pulled the Corolla into his driveway. It was hard to believe no one tailed him home; no one stood waiting in the house to pulverize him, and no one threatened his life anymore. Exhaustion pulled at his every muscle, nearly convincing him to nap right there in the car.

Amber drove her Mini into the driveway across the road behind him. She staggered getting out, and leaned against the car resting her head on folded arms. Josh couldn't believe she'd stayed with him the whole time – well, not when he was being questioned, but she did wait for him, held his hand, and leaned into him as they walked out of the police station. This thing with Saul wasn't over, but at least Josh wouldn't be hounded anymore. He pulled the car into the garage and walked back out again before the main door groaned shut. Amber stood at the foot of his driveway. She gave a tired smile and met him halfway up the drive.

Josh reached for her hand and gave it a squeeze. "What are you doing? You've been up all night. You should get some rest."

"As have you. I"–she looked over her shoulder at her

house–"don't want to be alone right now. Not after everything that's happened."

Something told Josh a lot more went on between her leaving the casino and showing up at Saul's. He opened his mouth to ask if she wanted him to come over, but if they slept all day and her dad came home... Josh wasn't sure if Mr. Miller would be okay with him back in Amber's life. Josh guided her up to his place. She could sleep in the spare room.

Josh fumbled to get the key in the lock. It slid home with a snap, the Cineplex fob dangling a moment before he opened the door. Both he and Amber froze on the threshold. The place was a disaster. Numbly, he kicked his shoes off and zombied through the foyer into the living room, avoiding the partially rolled up Persian rug, stray dining room chair on its side, and the barren, matching coffee table. He dropped onto the couch and buried his head in his hands, elbows on knees. The door swished shut and seconds later Amber sat beside Josh, her arms wrapped around him.

"I don't know if I've said it yet, but thank you." Josh shifted as Amber nuzzled her head into his shoulder. "For everything. I couldn't have done it without you. I still don't know why you did any of it – after all that's happened between us. I mean, I wouldn't have blamed you if you'd told me to shove it. I almost messed it up. I did mess it up." Guilt stabbed his guts and twisted its invisible knife deeper. "I won't let it happen again." If he had just played by her ground rules, the cops wouldn't have been involved and... *ah, who am I kidding?* He would have fallen right back into the trap again. Now, he had to admit to the world, not just his folks, that he had a problem. Josh shuddered.

"Hey, it's over now," she whispered, nudging him.

But it was far from over. He glanced at the room and closed his eyes. Josh wrapped an arm around Amber, wanting so much to believe her. They sank back onto the couch. One minute he sat there listening to her even breath as it flitted across his neck, the next sleep claimed him.

AMBER'S EYELIDS FLUTTERED. The scrape of wood against wood came again, pulling her from a dreamless sleep. Her cheek rubbed against satiny fabric and she opened her eyes. Josh's upturned living room lay stark before her. She pushed herself up and rubbed her eyes.

"Sorry," Josh said. "I didn't mean to wake you."

She blinked and watched him hip-check the dining room table over a smidge more to centre it under the chandelier.

"What time is it?" Amber fumbled for her phone then noticed it on the floor by her feet.

"Around two."

"Two? Oh no." Her dad was coming home for lunch. He'd freak out if she–but as Amber swiped to wake up her phone, it registered a text from her to her dad an hour earlier saying she didn't want to be alone and was over at a friend's. That she'd text later. "Did you…"

"What?" Josh looked over at her holding her phone up and waving it at him. "Oh, yeah. We fell asleep on the couch. I wasn't sure if you'd mentioned to your dad if you were home yet or what, so I thought it might be wise to text him something just in case he dropped in for lunch or tried to call you at the house wanting to touch base after you've been away for almost a week."

"Right. Thanks. I was expecting him home around lunch time." She got up and looked out the front bay window. Her dad's car sat in the driveway next to hers. *Did he eat or just tumble into bed?* He hadn't texted her – Josh – back, so he had to be out cold.

A chair clattered into place. Amber turned around and watched Josh waiting for her body and mind to catch up to the fact that she was not only awake, but over at Josh's place. She'd been so tired and worried about him when they got home. She hadn't intended to sleep over, it just kind of happened. Amber glanced at the text. She'd said that to him – she hadn't wanted to be alone. It was true. She slipped the phone into her back pocket. Josh set the last chair in place and turned to face her.

"How long have you been at it?" she asked.

"Over an hour. Just after I texted your dad." He rubbed his hands on his jeans then folded his arms surveying the space with a critical gaze.

Amber reached for the rolled-up Persian rug and worked at hauling it back into place in the middle of the room. Josh smiled and nodded, scrambling to help. The black lacquered coffee table lay lengthwise in front of the plush, cream-coloured couch where she'd napped – *with Josh?* Without a word, they both grabbed an end and set it back into position.

As they slowly made their way around the room from corner to corner setting end-tables to right and putting the few remaining nick-knacks in place, Amber realized Saul's goons hadn't actually destroyed anything. They'd made a hell of a mess, but what remained was intact. The Soji screen and several jade sculptures were gone, as well as all of the digital equipment: TV, stereo, gaming systems. Josh caught her analyzing the empty spaces.

"Yeah, they even took Alexa. Good grief, we had everything hooked up to that thing." Josh shook his head and sat down on the couch.

"What?" Amber asked.

"There's so little left. They took nearly everything they could carry."

"But I only saw the one truck out front." Amber sat down beside him, a little more space between them than earlier. She knew they weren't supposed to talk about the case, but she wasn't about to change her statement or the facts if she was ever called as a witness to testify against Saul.

"They arrived with two." He disappeared down the hall and did a cursory look into the bedrooms. "They even took my mother's standing jewellery box. Good thing she didn't keep anything of value in it." Josh rubbed his hands over his face. "You must have scared them off when you got home early. The exercise equipment is still in the basement. Doesn't look like they made it down there."

Amber tried to speak but nothing came out of her mouth. What did you say to someone who had lost so much for something so stupid? What did you say to someone you'd made a mistake with not once, but twice?

At least he's not in trouble anymore… well, other than with his parents when they find out. Amber backed through the living room toward the door. Whatever happened between them once they got back remained a fog in her mind. Her heart said one thing but her mind kept contradicting it.

"Well, it looks like you've got this. I should pull something out for dinner. Dive into my homework. I've basically got a long weekend before everything's due."

A pained expression etched across Josh's face.

"Don't forget to call your folks."

"I already did. Left a detailed message. They should get it tomorrow night when their cruise docks. They've got a night in an Alaskan lodge and then they'll fly back Sunday afternoon. That's kinda what I wanted to talk to you about."

"Oh? What's up? You think they're gonna throw you out?" That came out wrong. "I mean–"

His face blanched. "No, well, I guess they might."

Amber put her shoes and jacket on then stood and crossed her arms. The space between them chasmed. Her emotions refused to stop tumbling around inside her. She held her breath, willing them to stop.

He shoved his hands in his pockets and looked down at his feet. "I–I need to ask you for one more favour."

She frowned. "I'm not loaning you any money."

He cringed. It was insensitive but she'd done a little research about gambling addiction on the bus ride home last night when she couldn't sleep. The whirlwind of this morning had confused her – convinced her all that mattered was Josh being safe. Now he was.

"I need a lift. We can take my car, use the gas CAA put in it yesterday. I just need you to drop me off somewhere."

"Where?" Her heart spiked. She didn't know what it meant or what was going on.

He sighed, his chest and shoulders heaved with the force of it. "Port Hope."

"What? Isn't that like two hours away? That's four hours of homework time I desperately need…" Her voice trailed off. His green eyes flickered dark with a coming storm – more hazel than emerald. "What's in Port Hope, Josh?"

"The Canadian Centre for Addictions."

He finally looked up into her eyes. Amber's chest tightened.

"I can drive there and you can type on your laptop," he suggested. "We don't have to talk. Once I check in, I'm not allowed to have access to a vehicle. It's one of the stipulations. I need to get there before six or they'll give my spot to someone else. If I don't take this opening, I'll be put on a waiting list. I lucked out." He gave a half-laugh. "Someone cancelled and none of the others on the waiting list are able to go on such short notice. It's only an hour and a half's drive. Please."

Amber stopped herself from saying yes. She needed to think about this. The way he kept looking at her…

"Why," she asked.

"Why what?"

"Why are you doing this? Now?" A piercing ache vibrated

in her chest. If he was only doing this for her–

"I almost went online... to play poker – Vegas World Casino. I was cleaning my room, found my computer under my pillow. I had my login typed and everything, but I shut it all down and stuffed the laptop in the chest freezer."

Amber sucked in a breath, eyes widening.

"So, I started cleaning but my hands shook. I was jonesing. Bad. I'd gone all week only having made one bet, until the screw-up, and I still felt ashamed for giving in that much when you were trying so hard to help me.

"Amber, I really do need help. I see that now. When you were by my side you kept me clean. You reminded me constantly about the mess I was in even though I tried to play it cool. You held me accountable and I–" But he didn't finish his thought. "I owe my parents. I owe you – you gave up a week for me and we weren't even on speaking terms. I can't do this alone. I need help and the centre can help me. I don't want to be this person. I was never supposed to be this person. When I sold my truck... well, you know. It broke me. But our five-day road trip rebuilt a lot of what was missing. Please. I don't have anyone else I can turn to.

"If I wait until my folks come home... well, let's just say my dad thinks he can solve any problem, even mine. But he can't. I–I resent him for it. I know I'd lash out or purposefully find a way to go against him. I don't know why, I just know he pisses me off. It wouldn't work."

Amber stared at him trying so hard to read his mind – to search for the truth in his words. Her heart told her he was in this for the long-haul; her brain told her she couldn't trust an addict, or an ex, or her heart for that matter.

She nodded. "Okay. Let's do this. You drive, I work. I'll meet you in ten minutes. Her hand shook as she opened the door and walked across the street to her house. The quiet hung in the air. She checked in on her dad – totally zonked laying across his bed fully clothed – and then popped into her room. She grabbed her laptop bag and gathered what she needed for the next couple of hours before finding something to defrost in the sink for dinner later.

Back in the kitchen, she tossed together a couple of mega sandwiches, squished them into a container, and then wrote a quick note for her dad. Amber locked the door and walked back across the street.

She dropped onto the passenger seat, her stomach flip-flopping, heart summersaulting. Eyes closed, she leaned against the headrest.

"Ready when you are," she said, then dug out the sandwiches.

Josh nodded and gave her a faint smile, accepting her peace offering. "Thanks. I think we've still got some fruit in the back, maybe half a bag of chips."

Before he started the Corolla, Josh elevated his ass and took something from his back pocket. "Here. I know it doesn't make up for us not stopping at the Trading Post in Gravenhurst or for the grief I caused at Rama, but before I sat at the card table I did some nosing around in the gift shop." He handed her four business cards then buckled up and started the car. As they backed down the driveway, Amber read through them – twice.

She put them in her pocket and opened the laptop. Talking wasn't her strong point today.

For the first twenty minutes, until Josh had them heading east on Highway 401, an awkwardness hung thick between them. Josh had the radio on and the DJ spun a "way back" track. Both of them burst into song.

They took turns singing about why they were "too sexy" until they both sang the last line and broke into laughter. Amber went back to typing and even found a way to integrate the contact information from the four business cards.

She'd completely reworked the platform for the magazine

proposal. He'd been right. She had to watch out for perceived cultural appropriation. This zine couldn't come across as some random white chick feeling sorry for Indigenous Peoples. In fact, Josh's mom's now-missing collection of art from cultures around the world sparked a new idea. She named the mag Ally Arts – because that's how she saw herself, what she wanted to be…an ally.

The landscape went from a six-lane-highway in the middle of Toronto to a three-lane highway out in the sticks. At one point, as they neared Port Hope, Amber caught sight of signs for the Kawartha Downs Casino on the outskirts of town. Her chest constricted. She had no idea he'd be that close to temptation – that close to his vice. He was supposed to be getting away from those things not finding new ones. After that, she couldn't concentrate and she put her homework away.

Josh pulled off the 401 onto Highway 2 and headed south toward the water. They didn't actually get that far, but as Josh took the turn that merged Bramley Street with Dorset the tall hedges separating the road from the local estates gave way to a white picket fence and gate framing an old red brick house set back in the yard. He pulled in and took the car up to an enormous house with a circular drive around a stone fountain and four-pillared two-storey Roman architectural entry.

"This is a centre for gambling addicts?" Amber asked, awed.

"For all major addictions, actually. They did say it was a residential treatment facility, but… wow. I saw a few pictures online but I had no idea."

He turned off the engine and they sat there for a good ten minutes. Amber didn't want to rush him. It was only five o'clock and he had until six to check-in.

"How are you paying for this?" Amber finally whispered. It wasn't what she intended to say but she went with it now that it was out there.

"My tuition. I used my allowance VISA to place a down-payment and got the ball rolling for de-enrolling from my courses."

"What? Why? How long is the program here?"

"Most run about twenty-eight days. Depending on how things are going, I need to be open to staying an extra session if there's room. I'm kinda fucked up."

"But what about school? Won't this put you behind?"

"It's what I have to do. I'll work for my dad full-time, pay him and my mom back first. Then, maybe I'll take some online courses to finish off my diploma. I can learn the ropes from my dad just as well as going to school."

Amber clasped his hand and gave it a squeeze. Neither of them looked at each other – just up at the house. He really had thought about this. He was making positive choices for the future, his future.

"Don't forget that. You can get through this if it's something you really want. Something you're doing for yourself. Nobody else." She stressed the last words. The way he clung to her hand said so much and she held his just as tightly.

"I know. It keeps swinging though. One minute I'm sure I've got this – that I can beat it and get my life back on track. The next, I can't stop thinking about the tables, the track... the cops, the grief I've caused, and the mess I've made."

"You need to accept the past, work to change your habits, and look forward to the future," she said. It was something she'd heard from a TV ad, she was certain, but she meant it. "Do you want me to come in with you?"

He shook his head, took a deep breath, and held it. It burst out of his lungs moments later, breaking the quiet of the car. Josh reached for the latch, keys still in the ignition, and turned to face Amber.

He had so many things written on his face: fear, hope, worry, and something akin to the question in his eyes before they'd tumbled into each other's arms down the back hall of that bar after their pole dance...not quite a hunger but definitely something that set her skin on fire.

"I can't make any promises..." he started.

"Neither can I," she whispered. "I didn't want to leave, you know."

He squinted at her.

Amber's heart did its acrobatic routine.

"What are you talking about?" he asked.

"That night, at the casino. I told you I was leaving. I had turned back around to go in and get you. Determined to figure this out with you or, I don't know, try to be wonder woman and save the day. But my dad called." She looked up into his eyes. "Mom had a bad episode because of her MS. He was–he was frantic. Thought she might–" Amber still couldn't say it, but Josh squeezed her hand.

"You thought you were going to lose her. You made a choice. Hey,"–he clasped her other hand, too–"you did the right thing. If you hadn't left, I would've kept relying on you. I don't know what might have happened, but I don't think me going to the cops would have seemed like such a good idea. The fact that it all worked out still amazes me."

Josh kissed the back of her hand, then her forehead, grabbed his duffel bag from the back seat, and left the car. He didn't run or drag his feet. He also didn't look over his shoulder – just as she hadn't when she left him at the casino less than twenty-four hours ago.

She watched as he disappeared from sight and the front door closed behind him. Amber sat there, staring at nothing, for nearly fifteen minutes. She wasn't sure if she was waiting for Josh to run screaming from the building or for her to run screaming into it.

Finally, she shifted from the passenger side to the driver's, turned the key and went home.

EPILOGUE

28 Days Later

J osh walked down the stairs to the foyer and into the den-turned-office reception area.

"Well, today's the day, Josh. Congratulations." Terry, one of the lead advisors, leaned forward and handed Josh his box. The clear plastic container held his wallet, phone, high school ring, pack of Chicklets, and a folded picture. He put everything back in his pockets, including the photo. He knew the pic by heart but couldn't look at it. He'd wanted to say so many things to Amber the day she dropped him off, but nothing came out. It was like she ignored the fact that anything had happened between them – that they might still have a chance...

Josh let the thought trail off as he shook hands with Terry.

"Do you have a ride?" Terry asked, walking Josh to the door of the office.

"No. I'll call an Uber. Catch a ride to the station, and take the GO Bus home."

"I thought your parents were coming to get you."

"Yeah, things came up. I told them not to worry. It's all good."

Terry frowned and massaged his chin. Josh clapped him on the shoulder.

"Hey, I'm good. I'm ready. I wouldn't be leaving if I weren't, right?"

"Right. It's just that–"

"I know. 'It's highly advisable to be accompanied home after a period of stay'. You tell us all the time. But life happens, man. I feel good. No stops along the way, I promise. It's a two-hour bus ride. I got this."

"Yeah. Be safe man. Follow through on the program. Don't forget to check in once a week and remember, you can swing by and see us any time."

Josh gave him a salute and glanced at the grand estate house one final time before he slipped his coat on and grabbed his duffel bag.

Outside, the two-storey pillared porch did little to block the warm March sun. He squinted and pulled out his phone – no juice. The darn thing wouldn't even turn on.

"Figures. Guess I'm walking."

He stepped down onto the upper portion of the circular drive and caught sight of a car idling just past the stone fountain. A leggy someone lounged against the hood of a white Corolla with roof racks.

Josh smiled, hitched his duffel up, and walked over to the girl who'd saved his life. He chucked the bag on the drive by the front tire, turned, and lounged against the hood beside her – only a fraction of an inch between them.

"You came," he said.

"I did." A smile lit her voice. Neither of them looked at the other in some strange game of who might break first.

They both sat staring up at the elaborate building where

Josh had lived for the past month and soaked in the early spring rays.

"So, how'd it go?" she asked.

"Good. I'll never be done with the compulsion, but I know how to manage it now. Know there are people and groups out there who can help. Keep me honest. Accountable. They taught me how to work through an impulse and refocus my energy."

"Well, I hope you'll forgive me then."

"For what?" He looked first. Her eyes twinkled.

"For giving in to my impulse." Amber swung her body over and straddled Josh against the car, wrapping her arms around his neck, and pulling him close. Her soft lips caught his, nudging his face up before she kissed him the same way she had back at the bar that night, a month ago. He wrapped his arms around her and kissed her back. His heart sang and his groin stiffened. *God, she smells good.* He wanted to devour her, right there in the early spring sunshine on the hood of his car and he didn't care who might be watching from the windows of the house.

"You know, I'm supposed to go straight home."

She nibbled his earlobe and then nuzzled her nose into his neck. "Oh, dear. Well, then, I guess it's a good thing I'm driving." She laughed at the look on his face. "There's just one catch, mister."

"And what's that?"

"My mother wants to talk to you."

"She does?"

"In person."

"Oh. Is that a good thing?"

Amber pulled back but ground her hips into his, making him even harder. He cupped her ass, moulded perfectly by her tight jeans.

"I told her everything," Amber said, suddenly serious but no less intense.

"I see."

"Do you? I spent the better part of four years cursing your existence. She's concerned things might end badly between us, again."

"She is or you are?" Josh lightly slid his fingertips over her forehead and behind her ear, shifting a loose strand of silky hair.

"She is because I am."

He raised his eyebrows.

"But... she has a little more faith in you." She laughed. "Will you come?"

"To visit your mom?"

"Yes. Will come to the hospital for dinner tonight? Your parents said they'd be out at some Gala."

They likely told her they were advised not to leave him alone on his first night. Still, something told him Amber had been planning this long before his parents' plans got in the way...

"Yes, I will."

She smiled, gave him one last lingering kiss before breaking free and climbing into the driver's seat. A devilish grin lit her face.

Josh shifted himself, grabbed his duffel, and got in beside her.

They were going home... *eventually*.

ABOUT THE AUTHOR

Growing up in Ontario, Canada, M.J. was the only child of a single mom. M.J.'s passion for the arts ignited at a young age as she wrote adventure stories and read them aloud to close family and friends. The dramatic arts became a focus in high school as an aid to understanding character motivation in her writing. Majoring in Theatre Production at York University, with a minor in English, she went on to teach in both the elementary and high school divisions.

M.J. currently lives with her husband and young son. She keeps busy these days with her emerging authors' website Infinite Pathways, attending book fairs, and conferences as well as holding writing workshops and helping run the WCYR – Writers' Community of York Region.

Connect with M.J. online:

Author Website – www.mjmoores.com

Facebook – www.facebook.com/AuthorMJMoores

Twitter – www.twitter.com/AuthorMJMoores